CHRISTMAS IN HARPER FALLS

If I Had You

MARY J. WILLIAMS

About the Author

Want to know how to motivate yourself to write a book? Have your favorite football team lose the Super Bowl. On the last play. With an interception. The next day I was so depressed I tuned out all media. No TV, no internet, no newspapers — nothing. And I started to write. I'm still writing. As you can see, a little motivation can do wonders. Football will play a big part in my next series of books due out next year. And since I'm writing the ending? No interceptions. Guaranteed. Happy reading everyone.

Mary J. Williams

Please visit me at these sites and leave a message or ask a question.

NEWSLETTER: http://eepurl.com/bhFPPn

WEBSITE: www.maryjwilliams.net

www.amazon.com/Mary-J.-Williams/e/B00V041ET6/

www.facebook.com/pages/Mary-J-Williams/1561851657385417

www.twitter.com/maryjwilliams05

www.pinterest.com/maryj0675/

www.goodreads.com/author/show/5648619.Mary_J_Williams

More Books by Mary J. Williams

Harper Falls Series

If I Loved You
If Tomorrow Never Comes
If You Only Knew

Contents

Chapter One

SAM LAUGHTON EASED the rented four-wheel drive Porsche Cayenne onto the turnoff for Harper Falls. The snow was thicker now, cutting his visibility to only a few feet in front of the headlights.

Bad idea to leave Spokane. The car rental guy at the airport warned him of the incoming blizzard. His advice? Get a hotel room for the night. Harper Falls would still be there in the morning.

Instead of a friendly warning, to Sam the man's words sounded like a challenge. He was never one to take the safe way. When someone told him it couldn't or shouldn't be done, Sam barreled recklessly ahead. More often than not proving the naysayers wrong.

Some called it a stubborn streak; others cursed his otherworldly luck. Sam was okay with the stubborn part. As for luck — he made his own. From the time he was a small boy, he knew what he wanted. Money. Lots of it.

Not that he grew up poor. His family had been and still was, proudly middle class. His dad went to work every morning at seven, arrived back home no later than six. Dinner was on the table promptly at six-thirty. Mom happily took care of the house, her husband, and their three children. Look up the word traditional, the Laughton family was the quintessential definition.

Sam adored his parents. They gave him a warm, loving childhood. Even the town he grew up in was right down the middle average. Not too big, not too small.

His brother, Ted, married his high school sweetheart; his sister earned her degree, went back home, and now taught sixth grade at the same school all three Laughton children attended.

Sam admired them all, and visited whenever he could. However, it wasn't for him. He wanted money, glamor, and fame. He'd dreamed of excitement, travel, living in luxury twenty-four seven. And women. He wanted beautiful, sexy women on his arm—in his bed.

Next month he would turn thirty. In the twelve years since leaving home, he hadn't just fulfilled his dreams. He lived a life beyond even his teenage imagination.

Sam made his first fortune as a record producer. Artists sought him out; he was known as a star maker. Then he turned his sights on the movie industry. Untested, he knew no one would give him the artistic control he wanted. Therefore, Sam put up his own money to buy the screen rights to the hottest book in the world. In the right hands, *Wishes* had the potential to be that rare breed, a critical and box office success. Sam believed those hands belonged to him.

Investors weren't exactly lining up to back a first-time producer/director/screenwriter. Sam wasn't discouraged. He sidestepped the usual money resources. He used his considerable charms on anyone who would listen. This was not going to be a cheap production. He only wanted the best. Best locations, best actors, best costumes. Best music. The last item being what brought him to Harper Falls. Rose O'Brian.

Of all the women he knew, she was the only one who could say no with any conviction. She turned down his offer to share his bed. Boy, had that been a surprise. At the time, they were both single, healthy, sexually active adults. He knew that about her because Rose was not a shy little prude. When he asked her to share his bed, she told him in no uncertain terms that she liked sex. Sex with men. She thought he was handsome, and intelligent. Yet she refused. She just didn't want him in that way.

Sam's ego could take a little female rejection. He refused, though, to let her walk away from *Wishes*. Rose argued that she had never done an entire movie score. She didn't think she was right for the job. He didn't agree. In the end, he got his way. Rose's music turned out to be the perfect complement to his vision. If the critics were right, come February, they would both be rewarded with Oscars.

The last time they met in person was at the world premiere of *Wishes*. Rose's big ex-football player future husband acted as her very protective escort. Jack Winston trusted Rose. Sam, he wasn't so sure of.

Before becoming a billionaire security mogul, the guy worked in Hollywood as a bodyguard. Sam could take care of himself in a fight. Jack was bigger, but not by much. Still, when he kissed Rose, it was lips to cheek only. He didn't want to find out who was tougher; he had a feeling it wasn't him.

Rose half-jokingly invited Sam to spend Christmas in Harper Falls. The invitation was sincere; she just didn't think there was any chance he would accept. She was right. Under normal circumstances, he spent the holidays with his family. If not with them, skiing with friends. He never went away with a lover. This time of year was always about family, and friends. There were eleven other months to feed his voracious libido.

Sam cleared his schedule, ready to depressurize with his family, when word came from his mother that she and his dad wouldn't be home for Christmas this year. An old Army buddy was getting married. Almost sixty years old, this was his first time down the aisle. Sam's parents wanted to share in the holiday-themed ceremony. They were flying to Boston, and staying until after the first of the year.

Colorado skiing was an open choice. Then he remembered Rose's invitation. To be honest, he was intrigued by Harper Falls. What was the allure? From what he understood, the place boasted an array of people even a city ten times the size would be proud of.

Besides Rose, there were her two best friends. Dani Wilde, a Pulitzer Prize-winning photographer, and Tyler Jones, an artist on the rise. Sam even owned one of her sculptures.

Then there were the two billionaires. They brought a massively successful cyber-security company to Harper Falls. Why? They could live any place in the world.

Sam turned onto the main street. Apparently, Harper Falls shut down during major snowstorms. A few lights, from still open businesses, shined through the blizzard with an eerie glow, but there were no other cars to be seen. People wisely stayed home, out of the weather.

According to his GPS, the turn to Rose's house was at the other end of town. Sam had no idea what the condition of the road would be. She lived on a mountain. He looked around, wondering if one of the lighted windows was a hardware store. A set of chains might be needed to get where he was going.

Sam moved along at a snail's pace, his attention on the storefronts, not the road, when out of the corner of his eye he saw a flash of movement. What the hell? Reflexively, he slammed on the brakes, the back end of his car swerving left, and then right before the whole thing came to a stop crosswise in the middle of the road. Thank God for small towns and no traffic.

Sam opened his door, sliding out. He hadn't heard or felt a thump. Nor had he seen any more movement. Fearing the worst, he quickly walked to the other side of the rig. What he saw stopped him in his tracks. No blood. No broken body lying in the snow. Instead, he found a big, wet dog.

Unmoving, man and dog stood for several moments, staring at each other. Sam in amazement. The dog appeared to be unconcerned by the narrowly avoided tragedy he was almost a part of. His head cocked to one side, his mouth open in what could only be called a goofy grin.

He sat waiting. Waiting for what, Sam had no idea.

"You crazy mutt," Sam said, shaking his head. "If I hadn't noticed you at the last second, you would have been roadkill."

Sam knelt, his hand checking the dog's neck for a collar. Nothing. He turned, his blue eyes meeting big, brown ones. The dog leaned nearer, practically begging for a pet. Shaking his head with a chuckle, Sam obliged, smoothing back the wet hair on the big guy's forehead.

"Other than being soaked to the skin, you look like you're in good shape. Well-fed. Did you lose your collar and tags?"

Sam laughed again. Did he think the dog was going to answer? The big animal had intelligent eyes, but he doubted speech was among his talents.

"You go on home now. You've had your little adventure in the snow. I'll bet your owner is worried sick."

The dog gave him one more look before trotting off the road and down the sidewalk. Sam stood, his nose wrinkling at the smell of wet dog on his hand. He picked up some snow, scrubbing off a few hairs and the worst of the scent.

Climbing in the Porsche, Sam noticed colored lights outlining the window directly across from him. *Peony.* Even in the falling snow, he could tell the place would be a cheery haven. The sales clerk might be able to tell him his chances of getting up Crossfire Hill in his four-wheel drive vehicle.

Sam hopped into the cab. Convenient. He could get some information and pick up some flowers. Rose would be his hostess for the next few days. While the gifts he came with were more than adequate, a bouquet was never a bad idea.

Sam parked, turning off the ignition. Getting out of the cab, he didn't notice the big, grinning dog at the end of the block. Sitting. Waiting.

LILA FLEMING KNEW opening the shop on a day like today was an exercise in futility. The streets were deserted. In all likelihood, they would stay that way until tomorrow when the snowplows cleared the roads. Right now, she could be snuggled down on her couch with a cup of hot chocolate and that new mystery she'd meant to read for the last month.

When she spoke to her brother earlier that morning, Alex told her that's what he and Dani were going to be doing. Snuggling that is. Lila was sure that the lovebirds would find something more interactive to do than read a book.

She asked herself, *Why am I standing behind the counter waiting for customers who weren't going to arrive?* Because she was restless, that was why. She felt like something was about to happen, something big. What and when, she had no idea. The waiting drove her crazy.

There was always something to do when you owned your own business. *Peony.* If anyone asked, she always said the shop was what she knew. Back in Oregon, flowers had been the family business. From the time she was old enough to hold a garden hose, she helped water the plants, weed. Later, she graduated to running the cash register.

The sudden death of her mother and father in a plane crash was a shock from which Lila had never recovered. She was in college at the time, Alex in the army. His leave was short, just long enough to arrange the transportation of the bodies from Wyoming, attend the funeral, and jumpstart the sale of the business. At the time, Lila was in no state to take over. She was more than happy not to have the burden.

Sometimes she wondered how she finished school. From the moment she heard about her parents' death, Lila felt like she was walking around in a haze of disbelief. A phone call from Jack Winston was what finally snapped her out of her cloud of gloom.

Jack was her brother's best friend, kindergarten through twelfth grade. Alex joined the Army; Jack went off to play college football. Lila knew they kept in touch. That they talked about her had come as a big surprise. Jack asked her to come to Washington State. He and his business partner, Drew Harper, were moving their company to Harper Falls. It was Drew's hometown; his family founded the place near the turn of the last century. According to Jack, it was a great place to start over.

Lila didn't need much convincing. She needed something new. Something fresh. Flowers were all she knew; it made sense to open a shop. With the help of Jack, Rose, and all their friends, her business thrived from the get go. Last summer when her brother, fresh out of the Army, moved to Harper Falls, everything was perfect. Or rather, it should have been.

It wasn't that Lila was unhappy. She liked her life. Alex was safe, and in love. She had friends. She dated some very nice men. The problem was she once had dreams. Dreams that seemed unimportant after her parents died. Now, four years later, she wondered if maybe she gave up on those dreams too soon.

The bell over the door startled Lila out of her melancholy wanderings. Surprised, she turned to see who was crazy enough to wander out in this weather. She at least had an excuse. Not only did she own *Peony*, she could close up at any time. Her home was above the shop. At the end of her day, no snow boots were required.

"Good afternoon."

"You think? I haven't decided yet."

"Maybe I can help get you there."

Lila turned. She poured hot cider into one of the cups from a set made as a birthday gift for her by Tyler Jones, Harper Falls' resident artistic genius. It was difficult to believe she knew people like Tyler, Rose, and Dani. They were famous, celebrities. Not only could she wave when they passed on the street, they often stopped to talk. They had dinner together, met socially. They were her friends.

"Take this." She handed him the steaming mug. "Nothing bad can happen when you're sipping a hot beverage."

"I never knew cider was magical."

"It isn't." She twisted over the counter, coming back with something in her hand. "Unless you add a cinnamon stick. Now," she plopped it into his cup, "protection complete."

Sam laughed. His eyes sharpened with interest when he finally stopped being annoyed long enough to get a good look at the woman in front of him. Curvy. Oh, he liked curvy. A mass of brown hair streaked with gold and dark eyes shot with just a touch of green. She wasn't tall. Then again, she wasn't short. From where he stood, everything was just right.

"I know you."

"Have we met," he asked, certain he wouldn't have forgotten this beautiful woman.

"Nope."

Puzzled, Sam watched as she walked back behind the counter. *Nice,* he thought, appreciating the way her jeans molded a well-rounded butt. Normally, he was a breast man. When she turned, he couldn't help thinking — JACKPOT. Great ass; spectacularly filled out sweater.

"You *do* know my friend, Rose O'Brian."

He took the magazine from her outstretched hand. There he was, with Rose, at the premiere of *Wishes*. In the background, just to the left, the lovely blonde he'd brought as his date. Sweet Serena. The face of an angel, the mouth of a —.

"High class call girl."

"Pardon me?"

Sam looked at the woman in front of him. Was she a mind reader? If he were the kind of man to pay for his pleasure, Serena would have earned every penny.

"The article next to your picture mentions Hollywood's use of high-priced call girls to seal deals. I wondered if that was true."

The look she gave him was wide-eyed, innocent. The sparkle, the twitch of her full lips, told another story. This woman was a tease, in the best sense of the word. He hated when women came on too strong. The excessive compliments, the overly effusive fawning.

Sam liked to laugh. He had a feeling this woman would know just how to make him. He pictured the fun they could have during his brief visit to Harper Falls. Finding a sexy bed partner wasn't on his agenda, but he was flexible. Hopefully, so was she.

"Sam Laughton."

"I know." This time she grinned outright. "It says so right under the picture."

Sam smiled back. Oh, yes. This unexpected holiday just got a whole lot more interesting.

"Will you tell me your name? Or should I just call you gorgeous?"

"No."

"No, you won't tell me your name?"

"No," she clarified. "You can't use any cheesy lines on me. You can flirt. I like that. Save the icky pick-up chatter for when you get back to L.A."

"Paris."

"What?"

"I live in Paris, not L.A."

"Not the point."

"You're right." Lifting a finger, Sam made an x on his chest. "Cross my heart. No cheesy lines. I was serious about the gorgeous part, though. You are. Honestly."

Lila wanted to be cool. Act sophisticated. Not only was Sam Laughton, legendary ladies' man, in her shop, he lived in Paris. And not as in Texas. Her Harper Falls friends may be world travelers, she, on the other hand, was not. Visiting different countries, living in one, was a big part of her set-aside dreams.

"Lila Fleming."

Sam took her proffered hand, shaking it. Normally he would have kissed the back, his eyes locked on hers. Lila, the name suited her, might think such a move *icky*. He needed to rethink his moves. What worked with other women was not for Lila.

"Rose mentioned you were coming to town. I thought I would meet you at the party she and Jack are throwing on Christmas Eve. Having you come into my shop is a surprise."

"A happy one, I hope."

"Are you kidding? I was bored out of my mind. The snow is keeping everyone where they should be — at home."

"Why aren't you? At home," he clarified.

"I live up there." Lila pointed to the stairs in the back of the shop. "I became sick of my own company, even doing inventory sounded good. I was about to start when you came in."

Sam bit his tongue before he told her he couldn't imagine anyone getting sick of her company. Wow, his lines *were* cheesy. He realized he was getting lazy, or maybe his success made it unnecessary for him to dig for anything deeper. He liked women. They deserved more effort on his part. Thank you, Lila. From this moment forward, he planned on being more engaged when he flirted, more thoughtful. Not every woman was the same. This one? Straightforward was definitely the way to go.

"I stopped in to buy some flowers. For Rose."

"That's nice," Lila said. "Most women love getting them."

Most women. But not her, Sam thought. How many unthinking men brought her a bouquet? They would know she worked with flowers all day. She would take them with good grace, of course. Thanking her date, wondering why men had no imagination. What would Lila want? He would have to think about that for a while.

"How did you find me? In this weather, it's a wonder you could see to drive, let alone see my shop, if you weren't familiar with the town."

Lila carried on the conversation with her back to him, her head inside the refrigerated glass case that took up one wall of the shop.

"A dog. He walked in front of my SUV. Luckily, I wasn't going very fast. When I stopped, I was literally facing you."

"That dog?"

Sam looked over at the door to find *that* dog sitting on the other side. He seemed to be waiting. Well, hell.

"I looked for a collar, tags. Nothing."

"If he's lost, the vet might know him. Or he could have a microchip implanted."

Sam looked at the dog. The dog looked back at Sam.

"Where's the vet?" he asked Lila.

Lila put the finishing touches on the box. A pretty red bow, very festive, then handed it to Sam.

"A mixed assortment. Lilies, tulips, even a few roses. The colors are seasonal. As for the vet? She's just down the street. Unfortunately, like everyone else, she isn't there. She will come in for an emergency." Lila looked outside. "He's wet, probably hungry. Not emergency material."

"It is if some kid is missing his dog. Some Christmas."

Sam expected Lila to brush off the idea. So what if a little kid was worried about his dog?

Lila picked up her phone, did a quick search, and then dialed. She talked to someone Sam assumed was the vet, arranging to meet him at her office.

"She'll call as soon as she gets there. In the meantime, we should get that guy in out of the snow."

"I'll do it," Sam stopped her when she would have opened the door. "First, do you have any old towels? The second he's in here, he will be shaking the wet off. Unless you want it all over your shop…?"

"I'll be right back."

Sam didn't have long to wait. Lila was up and down the stairs in a flash, bringing a pile of light yellow towels.

"These don't look very old."

"They aren't." Lila shrugged. "But they're all I have. I'd rather wash them instead of my shop."

"Or maybe get new ones?"

"It won't break me," Lila laughed.

She had a great laugh. Natural, a little husky. It made him want to kiss that sexy mouth mid-laugh, catching the joy. Seeing if he would feel what she was feeling.

"Shouldn't we let the dog in?"

Great, Sam thought as he moved to the door. She caught him staring at her mouth. For a guy who prided himself on his smooth, easy manner around women, it was strange how easily this one was shaking his cool.

Cautiously, he opened the door. There was no telling what the dog's reaction was going to be. With his size, his rampaging body could do a lot of damage. He shouldn't have worried. This guy appeared to be a well-trained gentleman. Instead of pushing his way into the shop, he calmly walked in, looked around, continued over to Lila.

"Well, aren't you the gentleman?" she praised when he offered her a paw in welcome.

She knelt, shaking the outstretched foot. Lila didn't recognize him. People walked their dogs past her shop every day. If she'd seen this big, sweet-faced guy, she would remember.

"Let's not take any chances that he's going to remain so well behaved."

Sam took one of the large towels. Starting at the dog's head, he began the considerable job of drying the soaked coat. Lila noticed with pleasure that he was firm but gentle. Sam murmured words of encouragement, praising how well the dog was doing.

So, the big entertainment mogul had a marshmallow center — at least when it came to dogs. It was nice. Her celebrity crush hadn't turned out to be a self-centered jerk.

"There," Sam said, sitting back. "I rubbed the worst of the water off. You'll finish drying naturally in no time."

Sam smiled up at Lila.

"What?" he asked, puzzled by the bemused smile on her face.

"Nothing, really. I was just thinking. Don't you high-powered guys usually hire people to do this kind of thing?"

"Unfortunately, I left my dog dryer home." He winked. "This trip I'm on my own."

"Let me take those dirty towels. I'll hang them out to dry in the back room. Hopefully, I will be able to knock some of that hair off, before I put them in my washing machine."

"Do you have a bowl we can use to give him some water?"

"I do," Lila said as she gathered up the wet towels. "I'll bring it back with me. Won't be a minute."

Sam frowned at her retreating backside. Lila suddenly seemed stiff, a little uncomfortable. What changed while he dried the dog? Where was his sexy, smiling flirt?

"Any theories?" he asked his companion.

No answer came, but Sam took the look in those big, brown eyes to mean, as one man to another, he understood completely. Women could be a mystery.

After quickly dispensing with the towels, Lila took a plastic container she used to scoop potting soil, rinsed it out, and then filled it with fresh water.

What was wrong with her? She wasn't a blushing virgin feeling her first rush of sexual attraction. Sam Laughton was kind to animals. Why should that get her hormones racing faster than usual?

Maybe, because on top of the gentle way he treated the dog, he was outrageously good looking. Tall, the top of Lila's head just skimmed his shoulder. She knew what was under that bulky coat. Just last week *People* ran a whole page, showing Sam and his woman of the moment, enjoying the beaches in some fabulous tropical location. Those pictures showed a man who easily could have been in front of the camera instead of behind it. Broad shoulders, fabulous chest, one of those washboard stomachs that only seem to exist in the movies, or her dreams.

Then there was that face. Holy crap, what a face. Not a pretty boy, Sam Laughton looked like a man. Strong jaw, full lips, and cheekbones that were to die for. How could high cheekbones look rugged? Somehow, he pulled it off.

Lila opened the small fridge she kept in the back. Mostly, it contained water, juice, some diet soda. Nothing to feed a big, she imagined, hungry dog. There was half a sandwich, though. Her assistant left it there the other day. Meatball sub. Lila didn't think Agnes would mind giving it up, especially when she found out why; she owned two dogs herself.

Reminding herself that for all his shiny glamor, Sam Laughton was just a man. Lila picked up the water and sandwich, and reentered the shop. When he turned, smiling in welcome, she silently scoffed at her own silliness. Just a man? Hardly. At least not like any man she'd ever met.

She set the water down, stepping back away from the spray created by the dog's enthusiastic drinking.

"Wow," she smiled. "He really needed that. I thought he might be hungry. A meatball sub isn't the healthiest option."

She handed the sandwich to Sam.

"It will do in a pinch."

Apparently, the dog agreed. In no time, he ate his snack, drank down another bowl of water, and found a spot just right for a nap.

"Dry, rehydrated — a nice bit of food in his belly. That is one happy dog."

"Animals have simple needs." She looked Sam up and down. "Most animals."

"My needs are simple," Sam assured her. When she snorted in disbelief, he shrugged. Then grinned.

"Relatively simple. I like to be dry. I'm always happiest when my belly has something in it. Water is essential."

"And?"

Oh good, Sam thought, seeing the lovely twinkle back in her eyes. They were reentering the flirt mode.

"If I ask you about your supply of mistletoe, would that be cheesy?"

"No. Not cheesy, just ill timed. There was a big run on it this week. I'm all out."

"None hanging in the shop?"

"I tried that last year. It gave too many men the wrong idea."

"They all wanted a kiss?"

"Most of the guys were fine. It was the others that caused the problem. They wanted to grab any woman within a five-foot-radius. The mistletoe was taken down before closing."

"There are always a few jerks who ruin the fun for everyone else." Sam moved closer. "We could skip the mistletoe."

Lila tried not to smile. He looked so hopeful. That look did wonders for her ego.

"Where's your holiday spirit?"

"Oh, my spirit is just fine." Sam's eyes dropped to her lips.

Not today, fella. Lila was afraid if she let Sam Laughton kiss her, it might end up as a lot more. Her bed was up those stairs. Maybe they would get to the bed. Doing it in her shop wasn't high on her fantasy list, but with Sam, she had the feeling anyplace would be the right place.

"Rose bought a dozen sprigs."

"I don't want to kiss Rose."

Good to know, Lila thought.

"You'll be at the Christmas Eve party tomorrow night. I'll be there." Sam caught on quickly.

"We're bound to end up under one of those handy mandatory kiss makers. A dozen. Hell, I imagine by the end of the night, we might hit them all."

"Let's not get ahead of ourselves. How do I know you're a good kisser? Maybe you'll think I'm too sloppy."

"Are you?"

"I haven't had any complaints." Lila tilted her head, a questioning look on her face.

"Me?" Sam asked. "I hate to brag…"

"Oh, go on. You know you want to."

"If you insist. The first woman I ever kissed swore I was the best she'd ever had."

"And she was…"

"Twelve. I was a precocious ten."

Lila was fascinated. An insightful, if humorous, look into a young Sam Laughton

"Did this much older woman have a lot to compare you with?"

Sam shrugged. "Let's just say Marcy wasn't the kind of girl who waited for mistletoe."

"A year-round kisser."

"Equal opportunity all the way too. She taught my sister how to kiss."

"Your sister is…"

"A lesbian," Sam told her matter-of-factly. "Olivia wasn't certain at the time. She claims one kiss from Marcy sealed the deal."

"That must be rare."

"Having a lesbian sister?" Sam asked warily. He waited tensely for her to make some offhand homophobic remark. He wanted Lila to be better than that.

"A brother and sister getting their first kiss from the same person. That must be unusual, right?"

Sam relaxed. Sweet. She was so damn sweet.

"I'm not sure it's *Ripley* worthy. A little odd. Definitely anecdotal."

They were close. Close enough to kiss. Close enough to do a lot of things. Lila found herself wanting to give into temptation. Why not? Sam wasn't going to be in Harper Falls very long. When would she get another chance to take advantage of this kind of situation? A real life, bona fide sex god, wanted her. She wasn't naive. This was about more than a kiss. He wanted a holiday fling — with her. She wanted him to have her.

She leaned closer when the phone rang.

"The vet," she said.

Lila was disappointed and relieved all at once. She wasn't ready for Sam Laughton. She wasn't wearing the right underwear. Her body needed primping. Check her legs. Stubble was a no-no. Lotion. The expensive kind she saved for special occasions. So many things. She wanted to make what would be a once in a lifetime experience as close to perfect as possible.

Sam listened as Lila filled the vet in. Damn phone. Lila was about to give him his kiss, he knew it. She wanted more; he could tell. A little Christmas fling. Not what he planned when he accepted Rose's invitation. Lila was a very pleasant surprise.

"She is waiting for you." Lila took a sturdy piece of rope, tying it expertly around the dog's neck. He was very well behaved, but she didn't want to take the chance on him running off between here and the vet's office.

"Nice knot."

"I dated a sailor for about a month. He taught me all kinds of nifty variations."

"Kinky?"

"Studious. He was still learning. I helped." Lila handed Sam the rope. "I don't attract sexually adventurous men. Guys see me as the girl next door."

Sam led the dog to the door. He was halfway out when he turned back.

"Why does everyone underestimate the girl next door?" He gave her a look that said he never would.

"See you tomorrow night," Sam said with a smile. "I'll be looking for you under the mistletoe."

Lila felt her cheeks heat, glad Sam wasn't here to see it. Sometimes she blushed. Not always. It wasn't something she could control or anticipate. Experienced women didn't blush. Did they? She wanted Sam to rip her clothes off in a bout of mad, wild, no holds barred sex. Pink cheeks made men want to take it slow, be gentle. Or back out altogether.

Lila decided right then and there. She wanted one thing for Christmas. Only Sam Laughton could give it to her.

Chapter Two

"THIS IS NOT a permanent situation. Understand?"

Cooper looked at Sam with adoring eyes. They seemed to say, *Think what you like. I'm here to stay.*

"No. I don't have the room, or the time, for a dog. That's final."

The trip to the vet turned out to be a bust. She gave the dog a thorough examination. Like Sam thought, he was healthy, well cared for. Until recently, he must have had a good home. No microchip though.

"He's been neutered."

Even knowing it was for the best, Sam couldn't control a sympathetic wince.

"Men," Dr. Baine smiled, shaking her head. "You all have the same reaction."

"No guy wants to lose his balls, Doctor."

"Mmm." What else could she say? "I can't be sure he's had all his shots. If you want, I can give them to him again."

"Won't that harm him?"

"No," She gave the calm, happy dog a scratch behind his ear. "He would be fine. Better safe than sorry."

"He isn't my dog. There must be someone out there looking for him, right?"

"I don't know him," she said. "It's possible someone passed

through town, stopping for some reason. This guy doesn't seem like the runaway type."

Sam swallowed, hating to ask. He looked at the dog, then whispered, "What about the *pound?*"

Even though he spelled it out, he was afraid the dog understood the nasty word.

"Across town. The storm would keep some of the staff away. I'm sure there's a skeleton crew. Want me to call?"

"No," Sam said. It didn't seem right. Especially this time of the year.

"Leave me your contact information. If anyone comes looking for this guy, I'll let you know."

That settled they were now back in the SUV. The road to Rose's house was surprisingly well tended. Freshly plowed, Sam found the trip easy and quick. His companion stretched out in back, unworried.

Could a dog look smug? This one did. Even after the *this isn't permanent* warning. Maybe because Sam gave in concerning the shots. As the vet said, having him vaccinated couldn't hurt. The last thing he needed was the dog getting sick on his watch. That kind of guilt he didn't need.

"I never should have named you."

Sam didn't think it was right to keep calling him dog. He searched for something that suited the big guy, settling on Cooper in honor of his dad's favorite movie star. *High Noon, Pride of the Yankees, Ball of Fire.* He lost count of how many times he and his father would sit watching Gary Cooper. The good, the bad, and the dreadful. Didn't matter. Looking back again, Sam admitted the name fit. The dog somehow looked like a Cooper.

The heavy security gate, down the road from the house, didn't make Sam blink. Jack Winston made his fortune keeping people safe. Why wouldn't he do the same for himself and the woman he loved?

He identified himself; the camera and intercom verified his identity. A few minutes later, he pulled up in front of a house that looked like it was from another century. Nineteenth, if he was any judge. Grandma's house. Homey. Not the kind of place he pictured when he thought about the couple who lived there.

Yet on second thought, the wraparound porch, dark green shutters, bay windows, all screamed Jack and Rose. They were a modern couple. He imagined inside there would be every convenience known to man, or woman. The more traditional outside design was a good choice.

Cooper seemed to know they were at their destination. He sat up, an excited sparkle in his eyes.

"Better than spending your Christmas wandering the streets, right Coop? I understand there's another dog who lives here. Remember. We are guests. I expect you to be on your best behavior and play nice."

As usual, Sam was sure the dog understood every word. Cooper even nodded at him.

"Right. Here we go."

He barely stepped out of the SUV when the front door flew open, a red-haired, streak of energy rushing out. Right behind, Jack Winston.

Sam had just enough time to determine it was a giggling little girl when she surprised him by launching herself at him.

"Charlotte Marie," Jack cried out.

"Don't worry," Sam laughed, scooping her into his arms. "I have a niece about this age. She's always coming at me like that. The Laughton charm acts like a female magnet. Age is no obstacle."

"I appreciate you catching her. She's decided four is a big girl age. That means going outside even when her mother told her not to."

Charlotte, obviously learning how to use her feminine wiles at an early age, batted her eyes at Jack.

"Love me?"

"Always, you little scamp."

He snatched her from Sam, tossing her into the air. The ring of laughter reached the house, drawing a crowd of six women of varying ages.

"Starting a harem?"

"I was blessed with six older sisters, countless nieces, and a mother who could pass for a woman half her age." Jack gave Sam a warning look. "Hands off."

"Your mother, your sisters? Your nieces seem a trifle young. Your soon to be wife?"

"All of the above."

Grinning, Jack tucked his niece under one arm, extending his other. Sam took the hand, giving it a firm shake.

"Thanks for having me, Jack. You look like you have a full house. Are sure I'm not going to be in the way?"

"Go back to your mama, Charlotte." Jack set her down, giving her a gentle pat on the bottom. He waited until she was safely back in the house before turning back to Sam.

"I built this place to accommodate my ever-growing family. If one sister isn't giving birth, another is about to."

"All girls?"

"My dad and I are the only men on the Winston side of the family. Luckily, my sisters all married good men. Who have proceeded to repopulate with girls."

"You don't sound too upset by that."

"Are you kidding?" The big man with sparkling blue eyes gave Sam a friendly pat on the back. "I wouldn't have it any other way. Now, let me grab your bags and get inside where it's loud but warm."

"About that," Sam said as Jack reached for the back passenger-side door. "I brought an unexpected guest."

"So I see."

Cooper greeted both men with a sharp bark. That was a first, Sam thought. Up until now, the dog was virtually silent.

"I know that sound." Jack stood back, his hand making a sweeping gesture towards the snow-covered lawn. "Go on, boy. My yard is your yard."

Cooper leaped from the SUV, running around, rolling in the snow, scoping out the area. Finally, finding just the right tree, he lifted his leg.

"If I'd known he needed to relieve himself, I would have pulled over before we got here."

"Most dogs will hold it until you reach your destination. I take it you haven't had him long."

"It's a long story."

"On cold, snowy days, that's my favorite kind. Looks like your friend is done. Let's go inside. He can meet Edgar; I'll introduce you all around. Then we'll settle down with a hot drink for story time."

Sam took the box that was stamped with a pink *Peony* logo. He waited for Cooper to shake off his newly acquired coat of snow before following Jack inside. What greeted them could only be termed barely controlled chaos. Children ran, played. Parents kept a watchful eye, for the most part, happy to let them.

"What do you think?"

It was so much like the holidays when he was growing up. Sam felt a twinge. If he couldn't be with his own family, this was a nice substitute.

Sam turned to Jack and grinned.

"It feels like home."

LILA PUT AWAY her notes, the regret becoming harder to ignore. She wrote something every day. Sometimes pages, sometimes one line. From a young age, she recorded her thoughts, wrote stories. The only time she stopped was after her parents died. Her mother's encouragement was gone. The loving belief that Lila's dream of being a writer, wiped out in an instant. The muse that used to sit on her shoulder, whispering, was gone.

For a long time, Lila was sure it would never return. As time eased the pain of loss, the spark flickered to life again. Slowly, a bit here and there. Writing became a joy again. The dream of doing it full time was harder to regain. She was a businesswoman. Running *Peony* took all her time and effort. The yellow legal pads stacked in her desk drawer were filled with stories no one would ever see. Now when she wrote, it was no longer with ambition. She wrote because she had to, for herself.

Pushing back from her desk, Lila shut the drawer on her wayward thoughts. She had a party to get ready for. She planned to kiss a very sexy man. Hopefully, more than once. Looking her best was essential.

As a rule, Lila didn't linger in the shower. Tonight, she took her time. She washed and conditioned her long, dark hair. The body wash filled the room with the scent of vanilla. When she finally stepped out, grabbing a fluffy towel, she was smooth and silky from top to bottom.

Drying her hair was always a chore. Most days she didn't bother. A clip to hold it back and she was good to go. With thoughts of Sam floating through her head, she knew that would not do.

Lila pulled out her seldom-used blow dryer before plugging in the curling iron she bought last spring, only to forget about it until tonight. Out of practice, it took some time. When she was done, she stood back, critically examining her work.

Not bad. A little make-up, the right dress. She might not be able to compete with Sam's usual supermodel type, but those women weren't here. She was. Applying her eyeliner, Lila promised herself to do this more often. Why wait for a special occasion? It was easy to forget, in the day-to-day living of life, how good it felt to pamper and primp.

Her choice of what to wear was a no-brainer. In the back of her closet, tags still attached, was a dress. An impulse-buy one day when she was shopping with Rose, Dani, and Tyler.

The soft, jersey knit hugged her body like a dream, highlighting her curves in all the right spots. The forest green color brought out the flecks in her eyes that were exactly the same shade.

Her legs weren't long, but they were shapely. The dress hit her just above the knee showing off her nicely toned calves. Thank you, step class.

Shoes were a problem. In this weather, boots were practical. For tonight, high heels were mandatory. Again, easy decision. Being good friends with the hostess meant Lila wouldn't feel awkward showing up in clunky boots then changing into strappy sandals.

Lila gave herself one more look in the mirror, before heading out. Hair, nice. Makeup? Good — not clown like. Sparkly earrings, her mother's gold bracelet. The dress was a killer. She was as good as she was going to get. Hot. Yes, little Lila Fleming felt ready to seal the deal with Sam Laughton.

They could start with a kiss. She hoped they ended naked, sweaty, and highly satisfied.

"I KNOW YOU didn't expect me to accept your invitation."

Sam stood with Rose, sipping aged malt whiskey. His enjoyment of her home and family grew with each passing hour. The large, open living area was decorated with festive lights, illuminating banisters, mantles, doorways. Boughs of pine scented the room, a large fire crackling, adding to the festive atmosphere. His companion, her shoulder-length brown hair shining with touches of red and gold highlights, glowed brighter than any light. She was lit from within. That's what loving, and being loved in return, will do for you, Sam realized. It made a beautiful woman incandescent.

"No," Rose admitted. "When I invited you, I was certain this was the last place you'd want to be for Christmas."

"Should I apologize? Not only do I show up, I bring an uninvited guest."

Cooper and Edgar, Jack's large black dog of indeterminate breed, were getting along like old friends. A few tentative sniffs was all it took. Now, they were patiently letting three little girls decorate their coats with ribbons of various colors.

"Cooper fits right in. Knowing his story, I'd be mad if you hadn't brought him. As for you, my friend." Rose linked arms with him. "I said I didn't think you would accept. I never would have made the invitation if I didn't want you to."

"Ever regret turning down my many advances?"

"God no."

"Ouch."

Laughing, Rose squeezed his arm.

"I think your ego can take one woman not finding you irresistible."

"Mmm." Sam gave her forehead a friendly kiss. "It did make it easier when I needed to get on your case. If we were lovers, I might have hesitated."

"Ha," Rose said incredulously. "You wanted those songs for your movie. A little intimacy would not have stopped you. You bullied, Sam. Constantly."

"Didn't you write some songs that will live forever? Classics, Rose. *Unconditional* has been number one for two months."

"You don't get to take credit for that, Sam." Looking across the room, Rose's eyes got dreamy. "Jack was the inspiration. You should be thanking him. I know I do. Every day."

"I still say my gentle nudging helped."

"Gentle my…" She did a quick assessment of how many little ears might be around to hear Aunt Rose swear. Too close to call. "My rear end."

Seeing Sam's amused look, she explained.

"Little pitchers have big ears. They also tend to repeat everything I say."

Sam nodded. "Hence, rear end instead of —"

"That goes for you too. Curb the language while you're here."

"Got it. Gosh, dang and shucks only. I promise."

Sam mingled for the next half hour, his eyes constantly checking and rechecking the door. No Lila. He knew she was coming. Earlier when he was talking to Alex Fleming, someone asked about her. She was coming. Being Christmas Eve, she stayed open to catch the last minute shoppers.

"Sam. I didn't know you'd be here."

The enthusiastic slap on his back might have felled a slighter man. As it was, he did stagger forward. Unconcerned, Sam grinned, happy to see the man, no matter how he greeted him.

"Bobby."

At eighty-five, Robert Plank was robust, energetic, and as Sam's shoulder could attest, strong as a bear. His shock of thick gray hair would be the envy of a man half his age. He was friendly, a bit bawdy, and one of the richest men in the world. His money gave Sam the last boost he needed to make *Wishes*. Finding him at a Christmas party in Harper Falls, Washington was a big surprise.

"Thought a young stud like you would be spending the holidays in bed with a beautiful woman. Or two."

The last bit sent Bobby into gales of laughter, drawing smiles from everyone nearby. Bobby had an infectious personality, drawing people in as easily as he made money.

"I would have thought the same about you. Last I heard wife

number six was history, making you free to play the field."

"I do like a beautiful woman. Plenty around here. I'm mighty fond of that one in particular."

Sam looked to where Bobby was pointing. Dani Wilde? Really? She was a looker, no doubt. All that white blond hair, her emerald green eyes. Put those together with a shapely body and a face that could grace the cover of magazines. Sam definitely saw the appeal. From their brief conversation, she seemed intelligent, friendly. She was also engaged to Alex Fleming.

"Nothing like that," Bobby assured Sam. "Though I appreciate the thought. No, that sweet lady is like a daughter to me. We met up about four years ago and it was love at first sight. Platonic love. I couldn't be happier that she's found a good man. Unlike me, *that* is a woman who loves once and strong. Lucky for Alex, he feels the same. If I'm too old to kick his ass, I wouldn't hesitate to hire somebody to do it."

"He's pretty hardcore, Bobby."

The older man's usually jovial expression hardened.

"When it comes to those I love, son, so am I."

Sam didn't doubt it for a minute. He shook Bobby's hand before wandering through the crowd. And a crowd it was. Half of Harper Falls must be here. It didn't matter to him that he was a stranger in a group of friends. Sam was a social being. He liked his own company, sometimes nothing else would do. This, though, was where he thrived. He liked people, all types. They liked him back because he was genuinely interested. When someone talked to him, he listened. A talent that came naturally to him.

He particularly liked the company of beautiful women. Rose's friends qualified and then some. When that beautiful woman was also extremely talented, he couldn't resist. Dani Wilde was a respected photographer. Her work was diverse, one time in a glossy fashion magazine, the next a gritty Newsweek feature.

"I wanted to tell you how much I've enjoyed your work over the years."

Dani, her green eyes even more spectacular close up, smiled at Sam.

"I can say the same. Rose complained the whole time she worked with you. I think we can all agree your butting of heads was worth it."

"Now if I could only get her to agree to record for me." Sam leaned in conspiratorially. "She has a voice that would sell a million records. Add to it the way she looks, she would be a superstar."

"Look at her, Sam." Dani tipped her head toward her friend. "She is a superstar without putting herself out in the public eye. She would hate losing her anonymity. The attention she's getting for *Wishes* is bad enough."

"Seems like a terrible waste," Sam said. He hated giving up, even when he knew Dani was right.

"Nobody that happy is wasting anything."

Sam was about to comment when he heard the name he'd been waiting for all evening.

"Lila."

The enthusiastic greeting came from someone in the crowd. Sam wasn't worried about them. His gaze zeroed in on the woman standing near the door. Lila. She took his breath away.

"Oh, no you don't."

Not taking his eyes off Lila's curvy perfection, Sam frowned absently.

"Pardon?"

"Hey." Dani snapped her fingers in front of Sam's face making him lose focus.

"What?"

"Stay away from my future sister-in-law, Sam Laughton," Dani warned. "Your reputation precedes you. Lila is a sweet young woman who doesn't need a wolf sniffing at her door."

"I resent the comparison," Sam said mildly. He glanced back at Lila. Mouthwatering, every inch. "No offense, but how do you know *what* Lila needs?"

"Meaning every woman could use a little of what you have to give?" Dani scoffed.

"Not every woman."

"God save me from the overinflated male ego." Dani took a deep breath then sighed. "I'm sure you would give her a nice whirl, Sam."

"I don't whirl women."

"You know what I mean. Look around." She spread her hands. "There are at least half a dozen unattached women here who would jump at the chance to be your Christmas nookie."

"Nookie? Jesus."

"Lila doesn't have the protective gear to withstand your maneuvers. Pick someone else," Dani urged. Her eyes narrowed when she saw Jilly Underwood sauntering over. "Except her."

Sam wasn't interested in the angular blonde bearing down on them, or Dani's reasons for warning him off. Her warnings about Lila were another matter.

"Exactly what do you think I'm going to do?"

He took Dani's arm, skillfully putting a couple dozen people between them and Jilly Underwood. He recognized that predatory glint in her eye and wanted nothing to do with it.

"I'm not saying you would deliberately hurt Lila. You need to understand. She's lived a relatively sheltered life."

"Sheltered as in former nun?"

"Laugh all you want, Sam," Dani told him. "I'm not the only one who will take exception at your interest. Her brother knows how to kill clean and hide the body."

Looking close, Sam realized Dani was only half kidding.

"You think your fiancé is opposed to his sister having some fun."

"Let's just say Alex is protective. If you lived here, had plans to be around, it would be different. Dallying with Lila then skipping out the next day? Not good."

"Dallying and nookie in the same conversation. That's a first."

"I'm serious."

"I can tell," Sam said. That was the problem. What Dani had to say was completely ridiculous, laughable. Unfortunately, he was the only one laughing.

"She is over twenty-one?"

"Yes," Dani sighed, knowing where this was going.

"Fully functioning both mentally and physically?"

"Not the point."

"We can safely assume hymen free?"

Dani gave in. She had to smile, damn him. Too charming for his or Lila's good.

"She has no experience with men who are so... experienced."

Sam could have stated the obvious. So what? If things went according to plan, day after next he would leave town with a very happy memory and Lila would stay — a little more experienced — equally happy. He wasn't worried about her feelings. He knew for a fact, you couldn't break a heart in forty-eight hours.

LILA SAW HIM the moment she entered the house. In her entire life, she had never been so sexually aware of another human being. Pheromones, hormones, good old-fashioned lust. She tingled. Her skin. Inside, outside.

Sam Laughton put every other man in the room to shame. He made her want to do things she'd only read about. She smiled. She was sure he would be an expert at every one of them.

She thought it wise to skirt around him for a little while until she got better control of herself. This was, after all, a family party. *And* her brother was here. Alex was getting better at treating her as an adult. Watching his little sister being sexually aggressive might be more than he would handle.

Instead, she sedately sipped a glass of white wine, chatting with Tyler and Rose.

"Your mother looks lovely tonight, Tyler," Rose said.

Tyler nodded, with a happy look on her face.

"See that hunky guy at the punch bowl?" she asked.

"The tall, slender man with the salt and pepper hair?"

"That's him. Seems the new doctor in town stopped at the beauty shop where mom gives manicures. He was there for a haircut, took one look at her, boom, the rest is history. I would say the man's intentions are definitely honorable."

"How do you know?"

"Because." Tyler gave Lila a wink. "No man hangs around for over a month, not getting any, unless he really cares."

"You're sure they aren't…" Rose searched for a delicate way of putting it.

"Doing the horizontal mambo?" Tyler laughed at the look the other two women gave her. This was her mother after all.

"Mom spent too many years with a man who treated her like crap. She was lonely even when she wasn't alone. If Dr. YumYum can coax her into bed I say more power to him, and way to go, Mom."

Since the topic was already sex, Lila casually asked a few Sam-related questions. Just to satisfy her curiosity. If she was going to sleep with the man, and she was, better to be well informed. She wanted him to leave town with a smile on his face. She wanted to be… memorable.

"I read that Sam Laughton knows a thing or two about pleasing a woman."

"Ha," Rose laughed. "He could write a book. Volumes. Then teach a class using his own source material."

"Then the two of you…"

"Mamboed?" Rose shook her head. "Not me. The women I know who have, are practically legion. They like to talk, why wouldn't I listen? Not one negative review."

"None?" Tyler whistled. "Impressive."

"I know. It doesn't matter how good someone is in bed, he's bound to have one or two dud sessions. Even if it's just a woman with her nose out of joint. Not Sam. He's legendary."

"Good to know," Lila said, her heart rate elevating.

Rose and Tyler exchanged looks. They recognized an interested woman when they saw one.

"Lila, you need to get those thoughts out of your head. Now."

"What thoughts?"

Lila knew she was blushing; the heat in her cheeks was a well-known feeling. Maybe if she ignored her reddening face, so would her friends.

"You can't hide anything with that fair skin." Rose put a comforting arm around her. She wanted to be kind about this while still hitting her point home.

"Sam didn't invent the one-night stand; he just perfected it."

"Before you go any further, let me make something clear."

Lila stood up straighter; annoyed that even at her full height, in heels, both her friends topped her by several inches. To be fair to herself, Rose and Tyler weren't wearing flats.

"I think Sam Laughton is sexy. Who wouldn't? For anything to happen, the attraction has to be mutual." Mentally crossing her fingers, Lila outright lied to her friends. "That doesn't seem likely, does it? I'm wholesome. A glass of milk, if you will. Sam is lobster dipped in butter. Not an appealing combination, is it?"

This time Rose and Tyler didn't need to look at each other. Their thoughts were in perfect sync.

"Grab some water, your pants are on fire," Rose declared.

"Her nose is growing by the second," Tyler agreed.

"What?"

"Lobster and milk? More like sexy man meet sexy woman. Whoosh. Fireworks."

"You think I'm sexy?" Coming from these two women whom she both admired and envied, Lila found it the ultimate compliment.

"Are you kidding?" Tyler looked Lila up and down. "I came to terms with my lack of curves a long time ago. There was a time, my friend, when I would have killed for boobs like yours. Rose has nice ones, Dani's are great, but you, Lila are what straight men salivate over."

"Truth?" Lila decided confiding in her friends was the better way to go.

"Hey." Dani joined their little circle, her green eyes glowing, her cheeks blooming with color. Her lips nicely swollen.

"There," Lila pointed. "It would be obvious to a blind man what Dani and Alex were doing. See her eyes? The little smile on her face? She's been kissed. With purpose."

"Your brother knows his business," Dani admitted, her smile widening.

"No details, please." Lila sighed. "I've never looked like that, felt the kind of heat that sears your insides."

"Ah, Lila." Rose squeezed harder.

"You have. All of you. All the time. You don't need to be having sex to be having sex. I'd bet you anything, Rose, if your eyes met Jack's right now, I could guess what you both were thinking. Sex. When, where, how. The same for Dani and Alex. Tyler has ten years to make up for with Drew. I'm surprised they aren't in an empty room doing it as we speak."

"We aren't that bad."

All three women gave Tyler incredulous looks.

"Ten years *is* a long time."

"I don't blame you a bit," Lila told her. "It simply illustrates my point."

"But Sam…"

"Is the perfect man to help me out of my sexual malaise."

"Good word," Rose conceded. She looked at her two oldest friends, unspoken understanding passing between them.

"We need to get Lila laid. You," she pointed to Dani, "have the hardest assignment."

"Alex?"

"Right."

"Oh, God. Alex."

Her brother and his overprotective instincts did not bode well for her.

"Why does he need to know?"

"Trust me. I'm not going to tell him about his little sister's plans to be debauched by a legendary ladies' man." Dani shuddered at the thought. "If the subject *does* come up, I'll remind him about Portugal. He was a year older than I was, but he was miles ahead in experience. That should give him pause. Alex hates a hypocrite."

"Good." Lila smiled, grateful to her friends for their understanding and help. "Now," she said to Rose. "Please tell me you hung some mistletoe in an out of the way place."

SAM FELT LIKE a teenage boy. It was the last time he remembered sneaking around, desperate for a simple kiss. It was the last time he needed to. Or wanted to.

Here he was in his thirtieth year. He worked hard. Charmed, bulldozed, and hammered his way to the top of an ultra-competitive business. He didn't want his sex life to be difficult. He spent his days pursuing clients, romancing investors.

At night, he was happy to sit back and let the women come to him. He liked their company for a few hours. A few weeks at the most. A few tried to manipulate, play hard to get. Sam walked away, no hard feelings. He told himself it was because he didn't have the time. The truth was he didn't find any of them worth the effort. Until now.

Lila. She slipped through the crowded party like an elusive nymph. He knew she was teasing, at times her smile directed at him. He followed, not too close, enjoying the lightness, the fun of the chase. He wasn't going to grab her in front of everyone; she knew that.

They sipped their drinks, made small talk, laughed. All the while staying away from each other. Letting the anticipation build. He was practically giddy. *For a kiss.*

"I thought about a career in the movies. Everyone in Harper Falls says I'm prettier than any of those Hollywood starlets."

He knew the woman, whose name he'd already forgotten, was talking to him. Billy, Tilly. Something like that. Whatever she was saying was lost on him, his concentration focused on Lila, who chose that moment to beckon him with a discreet crook of her finger.

Sam grinned, starting toward the door Lila exited through. He only got a few steps when he felt five sharp claws digging into his arm, his thick cream-colored cashmere sweater providing little protection.

"You really need to remove your nails, lady."

"But…"

Sam didn't speak again, giving her a look that made more than one high-powered producer cower like an inexperienced newcomer. Jilly was no match for the intense blue gaze. She snatched her hand back, watching as Sam crossed the room without a backward glance.

"Want a piece of friendly advice, Jilly?" Seeing the wary expression in her longtime enemy's eyes, Rose smiled reassuringly. "No tricks, no nasty comments, I promise."

"Fine."

"Stop trying so hard. You are an attractive woman; you have money. Let those things work for you."

"You think I should buy a man?"

Rose realized the other woman was considering it. Oh, boy.

"No, Jilly. I think a change of scenery. New blood. Harper Falls has always been too narrow-minded to appreciate your... *unique* brand of charm."

"I do have a cousin in Dallas."

"Texas? All those cowboys and oilmen? Perfect."

"Unique charms?" Dani asked. She and Tyler, after not so discreetly eavesdropping, joined Rose.

"How would you describe them?"

"Nonexistent?" Tyler offered.

"If it gets Jilly out of town, I would tell her she could charm the birds from the trees. I'm tired of her showing up at my parties. She brings down the fun factor exponentially."

"Mmm," Dani shook off thoughts of Jilly Underwood. "Sam has risen in my estimation. He brushed that parasite off without a second thought. If asked, I doubt he could remember her name."

"The way he's been scoping out Lila, I wonder if he knows his own name. Can you feel the sexual chemistry between them?"

"Are you kidding? I thought that last look was going to leave a trail of scorched hardwood."

Rose sighed, linking arms with her friends.

"We are doing the right thing? Backing off, not interfering?"

"She's an adult, Rose." Tyler couldn't keep a touch of worry from creeping into her voice. "He wouldn't hurt her? Physically, I mean."

"God, no. Sam is one of the good guys."

"Enough. I'm officially letting my little chick fly from the nest." Rose lifted her glass.

"To mind-blowing sex, long may it reign."

"I SEE YOU found some mistletoe."

"I found some mistletoe hidden from public view."

Sam entered the room. An office? Den? Like every other room in the house, there were tasteful touches of the holiday season. Boughs of pine decorated the mantle above the gas fireplace, filling the room with its earthy scent. Lights twinkled in the windows, welcoming those inside and out.

Sam didn't care about any of that. Take away the glitter, the shine. Lila could light up any room with just her smile. Right now, it was turned on him — he was dazzled. He felt an unfamiliar catch in his chest, ignoring it in favor of the feelings she generated in another part of his body.

Lila waited for Sam, letting him cross the room at a slow, almost predatory pace. This was something she had waited for. Not only since their meeting yesterday. Most of her life. A teenage girl, writing flowery love stories about things of which she had no real knowledge. When she was thirteen, all her stories ended with a kiss. This one, she hoped, would go much further. A bed, two naked bodies, afterglow.

She wasn't expecting happily ever after. When Sam left town, she wanted happy memories. Multiple orgasms, please.

"I like that look on your face."

Sam was closer, only a few feet away.

"How do I look?"

"Sexy. I want to eat you, and then go back for a second helping."

Lila laughed, a little surprised by its husky quality. That was new. Like the way Sam made her feel. New — exciting.

"I meant, how am I looking at you?"

This time when Sam spoke, he was closer, right beside her. She could see the silvery sparks in his clear, blue eyes. She noticed a slight stubble coming through the close shave he gave himself earlier. And his scent. Clean, masculine. She wanted to lick his neck, curious if he tasted as good as he smelled.

"You look like you want what I want."

"Tell me," she breathed.

"Us." Sam moved in, his mouth hovering close to her ear. "Naked."

Lila gasped.

"I can feel it. Jesus, I haven't touched you and I know how good it will be."

"I doubt Rose would appreciate us taking advantage of the empty room. You never know when a guest might come in and catch you... decking my halls."

Sam laughed, the heat of his breath sending shivers through her body. His mouth grazed the curve of her ear as he whispered, "You want to trim my tree?"

"Yes."

"Unwrap my package?"

Sam slipped an arm around Lila's waist, his hand running up and down her back. He gave her neck a light, teasing kiss.

"Had enough?"

Lila tipped her head, encouraging his lips to taste.

"Aren't we just starting?"

"Oh, lovely Lila, you have no idea."

Sam kissed along her jaw, her check, the corner of that full, tempting, slightly parted mouth.

"I meant Christmas metaphors. Had enough?"

Lila looked up. Sam did the same. Mistletoe.

Without another word, their lips met. Their worlds exploded.

Sam knew how to kiss. He prided himself on his finesse. Not too hard, not too soft. The proper turn of the head, the touch his tongue against his partner's. He didn't thrust; he coaxed. The pleasurable hours he spent perfecting his technique. There was a time to be an animal, kissing a woman was not it. The second his mouth touched Lila's, experience flew out the window. This was primal. Ten seconds in, he knew without a doubt — this was better.

Lila's head swam. This wasn't a kiss. She knew what a kiss felt like. Pleasant, warm. A prelude to pleasant sex with a pleasant man. No, this wasn't anything like that. Sam... possessed her. Took control. Pushed her to someplace she never dreamed existed.

She wasn't worried about bumping noses, or when to breathe. She didn't care if she ever breathed again.

"What are you doing to me?" Sam pulled back, resting his forehead against hers. His breathing was ragged, his heart pounding like a jackhammer.

"Me?" Lila asked, amazed any words were possible. "You did this. I've never... I don't..." Apparently, words were possible, just not coherent ones.

"Together." Sam took her mouth again, making long strokes with his tongue along hers. "Us, combined."

"Yes."

Lila became the aggressor. She didn't want to talk — she couldn't. She didn't want to analyze. This felt too good. Right now, she wanted to feel.

Threading his fingers through her hair, Sam let the kiss go on and on and on. Lila tasted like the headiest wine. Subtle, intoxicating, irresistible. He couldn't stop sipping, taking more until his head spun, his body primed to take the next step. To take her.

"God, Lila."

She needed to touch him, feel the heat of his skin against hers. Sliding her hand under his sweater, her knees weakened. His back was all smooth-skinned muscle. Long, lean. Hot. Her fingers burned as they explored, teasing the waistband of his jeans. Would his butt feel this good? The temptation was too much. One hand ventured under the denim, seeking.

"Stop."

Sam jumped back. He couldn't take any more. One more minute —

less. He could have her dress up, her panties down in a heartbeat. There would be no turning back after that. Tempting. He shook his head. No, they weren't doing this here.

"Let's go."

"What?"

Lila looked at her hands, wondering why the palms weren't scorched black. With the sudden removal of all that heat, she felt cold — confused. Go? Go where?

Sam smoothed back her hair. He knew how she felt. His arms felt empty without her, strangely bereft, if that sort of thing was possible. Cautiously, he pulled her close, rubbing his check against the silk of her hair.

"Your place, Lila. Let's go to your place."

"I'm staying with Alex and Dani tonight. Christmas Eve."

"Right." Family. Sam hated messing with that.

"Alex will understand."

Sam chuckled. His libido was under control enough for him to see the humor in her observation.

"Understand that you would rather spend the night having sex with a virtual stranger? I doubt it."

"You're not..."

Lila was going to say he wasn't a stranger. He was. They met just over twenty-four hours ago. Had one conversation. Spent the last ten minutes making out. She *didn't* know him; it only felt like she did.

"Tell you what." Sam straightened her dress, doing the same for his clothes. "Go with your brother. Have a nice Christmas morning. I will call my family, and do the whole present opening thing here."

"All those little girls?" Lila wondered if he knew what was about to come.

"Kids make it special." Sam grinned again. "By noon, I will be ready for a break."

"Me too," Lila said, knowing where he was going. *Hoping.*

"Twelve-thirty, your place. We can take Cooper for a romp in the snow; tire him out. Then spend the rest of the day in bed."

"My bed. You and me." Lila didn't want any loopholes or crossed wires.

"Naked." Sam gave her one more thorough kiss, and then stepped back well out of range.

"Dream of me."

Lila watched Sam leave the room. She lifted her fingers to her mouth. It felt different. She felt different.

Dream of me.

It was funny. Something she could never tell him. Lila was afraid she had been dreaming of Sam Laughton her entire life.

Chapter Three

"MERRY CHRISTMAS, LILA."

"Merry Christmas, Alex."

Lila gave her big brother a hug. It was the first time in years they were spending the holiday together. Alex joined the Army right out of high school. He came home that first year. She remembered laughing at his buzz cut. All his lovely, thick hair gone. He wore it that way for the next ten years, until last spring, when he abruptly left the military. The reasons were still sketchy, at least to Lila. That was fine. She had her brother home, safe and sound. Even his hair was back.

"I thought about getting you a blow dryer," Lila teased, handing Alex his present. "You haven't needed one for so long. Then I realized you can use Dani's."

"Mmm," Alex laughed. His eyes lit up when the love of his life entered the room. "It was high on my list of reasons for asking her to marry me. Now you know, sweetheart. I only want you for your blow dryer."

Dani set down the tray, handing Lila a steaming cup of hot chocolate. The little marshmallows bobbed up and down, slowly melting into the liquid. Yummy.

"I suspected."

Dani settled next to Alex, her hand resting on his leg. It was an intimate gesture, natural, loving. Lila felt an unaccustomed twinge of envy. *Where had that come from?* She didn't want a man long-term. Someday, of course. Not yet. She was only twenty-five. There was plenty of time to find love.

Sam Laughton's face flashed through her brain. What? No. Sam was for fun, nothing more. She was meeting him later. *That* was why she thought of him. Love and Sam did not now, nor would they ever, go together.

"Hey." Alex waved a hand in front of Lila's face. "Earth to Lila. You looked a million miles away. Why are you blushing? What exactly were you thinking about?"

"Nothing in particular," Lila assured him. Her eyes met Dani's knowing gaze, making her blush deepen.

"Now I *know* something is going on. You look like a beet. A guilty one."

"I…"

What could she say? *Alex, I'm about to have a brief, torrid affair.* Wouldn't that go over well? She gave Dani a pleading look.

"Alex," Dani said, drawing his attention. "I know from experience that older brothers love to tease. I think this time you might want to give it a pass. Unless you want the details of your sister's sex life."

"What?" Alex exclaimed, obviously horrified at the thought. "No. Absolutely not."

"Then let's finish opening our presents. Mom and Dad are expecting us for a late brunch."

"Are you coming?"

Dani almost choked on her drink, her snort of laughter sending the liquid spilling onto her lap. Alex jumped up to get a towel, leaving the two women alone for a moment.

"After all this, you better be coming," Dani chuckled again. "Over and over and over again."

Lila's blush traveled down her neck. She might be embarrassed, but she was able to join Dani's laughter. Damn straight. She was tired of talking about it. She was ready for Sam Laughton.

COOPER RACED THROUGH the snow, his golden coat gleaming in the sunlight.

Christmas afternoon turned out to be beautiful. Clear blue skies beckoned them with an invitation to play. The man, woman, and dog were happy to comply.

"He loves being out here."

Lila watched as Cooper jumped into a particularly deep drift. He disappeared for an instant before popping back out, shaking off the snow. He checked, making sure Sam was still with him, and then bounded back into the pristine field. The dog left a big, happy trail in his wake.

"He loves being with you."

"I'll admit, he's growing on me," Sam said.

"Does that mean when you go, he goes with you?"

"It means I like him. I don't have room for a dog in my life. I travel too much; my place in Paris is too small." He shook his head with reluctance. "No, Cooper will make someone a great companion. Not me. *You* on the other hand."

Lila thought about it. Cooper would be a lot of work. He would also be a lot of fun.

"Why not?"

"Really?"

"Sure. A woman living alone? I have a security system, state of the art. A dog would be one more layer of protection."

"Then I could visit," Sam ventured. "Both of you."

Lila didn't answer. When he left town that would be it. Lila would not spend her time hoping Sam would find time to pop in for a day or two, leaving for months, even years at a time. They would have today. That was all.

She took Sam's hand, pulling until they fell backward.

"Snow angels."

Sam let Lila change the subject. What was he thinking? Not even out of town and he was hinting about coming back? Crazy. Completely unrealistic. She was right not to answer. They were supposed to have some fun, move on. There was no future. Not for him and Lila.

He flapped his arms and legs, laughing like a kid. Lila did the same. Cooper joined them, alternating between licking one face, then the other. This was what he wanted, Sam reminded himself. Light, easy. No promises. No strings. Not to Cooper. And Lila? He felt that odd clenching around his heart again. Damn it. Especially not to Lila.

"YOU WERE RIGHT about wearing Cooper out. A little water, some kibble. He's out like a light."

An afternoon spent frolicking in the snow left their furry companion happy, and ready for a nap. The corner of her apartment was now his. Lila would get a regular bed later, for now a thick blanket did the job. It was as though Cooper knew he was home. He circled once, twice, before curling into a contented ball. His light snoring followed within minutes.

Lila was too full of anticipation to feel sleepy. Add a few nerves, she decided. Wasn't it only natural? She wanted this; it was going to happen. Sam made her mouth water and her knees weak. He was also much more experienced. She didn't want to be a big, fat disappointment.

Lila could see it now. As Sam wrote his memoirs, thinking back on his many sexual escapades. The best he ever had? Hard to say. A toss-up between that redhead in Monte Carlo and the blonde in St. Tropez. The worst? Easy. That little brunette in Harper Falls.

"What are you thinking?"

Sam stood in front of her, so handsome, so sexy. His dark hair slightly ruffled after removing his knit cap. The sweater he wore, oh boy, could he wear a sweater, was that amazingly soft cashmere again. This time baby blue, almost the exact color of his eyes. Her eyes fell on his smiling mouth, making her thoughts wander. What would he do with those lips? How were they going to feel on her sensitive skin?

"My thoughts are kind of a jumble. All over the map."

"Nervous?" He smiled reassuringly.

"A little."

"Excited?"

"You have no idea."

"I think I do." Sam grazed her mouth with a mere wisp of a kiss. "I feel the same."

"Excited? I believe that. But nervous? Come on."

"I want this to be good for you. Better than good." Sam took her in his arms, swaying to a silent tune.

"There's this little spot, right here." He touched her temple, sliding his finger a little to the left of center. "I want the memory of tonight seared in. You will never forget me, Lila."

Lila stared into Sam's eyes, mesmerized by his words. Thrilled that he wanted to be a part of her — always. He barely touched her and he already had his wish. She would never forget this night.

Not letting her go, Sam bent, and picked up his phone. He tapped a few keys, sending a soft, bluesy melody floating into the room. She smiled. Silly man.

"I don't need romance."

Sam held her gaze, his eyebrows arching up.

"I do."

Sam led Lila into a slow, easy dance. He wasn't lying. He wanted tonight to be different from his usual encounters. Heat, yes. Passion. They were normal. The need for something extra never came into it. Until now. If he ripped the clothes from her body, taking her here with little preamble, it would still be special. Because it was Lila.

"Sam? Is something wrong?"

Yes. She was getting to him. In one afternoon. No, that wasn't right. Lila got to him in the first five minutes. Downstairs in that little shop she made him want her — want more. What it all meant, he didn't want to think about. Not tonight.

"I need to kiss you."

Lila smiled. Bright. Beautiful.

"There's nothing wrong with that."

Standing on tiptoe, she wrapped her arms around his neck, touching her mouth to his. She smiled again when she heard him groan. Her nerves melted and so did she. Luckily, Sam was there to sweep her into his arms.

"I plan on spending the next few hours getting to know every inch of your delectable body." He kissed her again with breathtaking thoroughness. "Any objections?"

"Just one. We have on too many clothes."

"Easiest fix in the world."

Ten long strides had them by her bed. Sam put her down before taking the hem of her shirt.

"Lift your arms."

Lila followed his command. A second later, she stood before him in her favorite red lace bra.

Sam traced the edge of one cup.

"That color makes your skin look like rich, silky cream." He leaned down, his tongue touching the area just above his finger. "Mmm. Sweeter." He tasted again. "Smoother."

Lila swayed. She reached out, frowning when she encountered cloth, not man.

"Take this off. Now."

Sam whipped the sweater over his head, bringing her hands to his bare chest. They both sighed with relief. That was better. He reached around to unfasten her bra, blindly tossing it away. He put an arm around her waist, pulling her until they were pressed together. Then he kissed her again.

It was almost too much. Lila was on sensory overload. Sam's kisses made every other man's attempts seem awkward and immature by comparison. The perfect blend of hard and soft. When his tongue entered, playing a sensuous game of pursue and capture with her own, Lila wondered if she would come from only a kiss. Intense. All consuming. She wanted it to go on forever.

Sam backed her up, pushing gently when her knees hit the mattress. Before she completely settled, her jeans, panties and socks joined her bra, forming a heap on the floor.

"There you go."

He stood back, taking in the view.

Lila wasn't used to being stared at. Especially when she didn't have a stitch of clothing on. *Don't blush*, she begged herself. Not now. Not when every inch of her was open, vulnerable. There would be no hiding it.

As that last thought raced through her mind, Lila felt the telltale heat rush through her cheeks.

"Turn off the lights," she pleaded.

Sam smiled, thinking he understood.

"Are you getting shy on me?"

"No, I…"

Damn, the red was spreading like wildfire. Down her face, her neck, the top of her chest. Think, Lila. Say something before he realized what a hick he was dealing with. Sophisticated, experienced women do not develop full body blushes during sex.

"I don't like looking at naked men."

Lila wanted to slap her forehead. She wanted sophisticated? That was a huge fail. She sounded like an idiot. Why would any woman with half a brain not want to look at a naked Sam Laughton?

Sam paused in the middle of unbuttoning his jeans, a puzzled frown on his face.

"You want the lights out so you don't have to look at my —"

"Thing."

Lila's eyes widened in horror. *Thing?* Cock, damn it. Penis. Dick. She had a grocery list of choices. She picked thing. What was wrong with her? Grabbing the quilt, she pulled it over her body rolling until she was bound tighter than a mummy.

"Lila, honey, what is going on?"

"Nothing." Her voice was muffled but easily understood. "You should go, Sam. I've made a mess of this. Sorry."

Close to tears, Lila waited to hear the sound of Sam's retreating footsteps. Instead, the mattress dipped, his body settling next to hers. No, no, no. Go away. Full blush and tears? She looked like a wet, blotchy, mess. What a turn on.

"It must be hard to breathe in there."

"I'm good."

She heard him chuckle. Now she was a joke? This was getting better and better.

"Lila." She felt Sam pulling the end of the quilt, gently unrolling her. "Come out and tell me what's wrong."

As ridiculous as this had become, Lila couldn't bring herself to crawl out of the hole she'd so awkwardly dug. She clutched at the material, holding on for dear life.

"Why are you still here?"

"Why would I leave?"

"Because I'm a mess." Resigned, Lila dropped the cover from her face. "Look at me. Red from head to toe." She hiccupped. "Wet face, runny nose. A real sexpot."

Deciding this was not the time to laugh, Sam smothered the urge. He gathered the distraught Lila into his arms. Using the end of the quilt, he wiped away her tears then lightly kissed the end of her nose. *Sexpot?* Not at the moment. Just a woman in need of comforting.

"Tell me what happened," he smoothed back her hair. "I thought everything was going great. Did I frighten you? Are you really afraid of seeing my thing?"

"Oh, God." Lila couldn't burrow back under the quilt; so instead, she hid her face in the crook of his neck. "I can't believe I used that word. Penis. I could have said cock or dick."

"All applicable."

"I blush."

"I'm going to need a little more information, honey. You blush. I imagine most people do."

"Sure. Delicate little flushes. I've seen those women. I hate those women." Deciding she might as well get it over with, Lila threw off the last of her cover, revealing her body.

"Look."

"If you insist."

Normally, Sam's exaggerated leer, the way he wiggled his eyebrows, would make her laugh. Right now, she couldn't summon up even the weakest of smiles.

"No, Sam. Really look. I'm red. Top to bottom. Like an over-boiled lobster."

Sam laughed, garnering a horrified look from Lila. When she tried to cover up again, he stopped her.

"Lila." Sam lifted her chin. "Look at me. Please."

When she did, Sam could see the hurt and embarrassment. He felt a little squeeze around his heart. Sympathy and something deeper. Oh boy. He might be in trouble.

"I wasn't laughing at you."

"Why not? I look like a clown."

"I hate clowns. Wouldn't be close to one for anything. You, on the other hand. There is no place I would rather be."

"Right." Lila was not convinced.

"You gave me an out. Did I take it?"

"No. But—"

"I laughed because the idea of me ever finding you anything but hot and sexy is ridiculous."

Sam ran a finger across the bridge of her nose. He lightly caressed her cheek.

"I noticed your blush."

"You'd have to be blind not to," Lila snorted.

He ignored her.

"I watched as it tinged the top of your chest," his fingers followed the path of his words. "Moved to your breasts. Spectacular, by the way. I practically salivated to see if it would reach these wonderfully hard tips."

Without warning, Sam bent to kiss her nipple, his tongue bathing the end with an all too brief taste.

A moan slipped from Lila's mouth.

"You covered up before I found out and now the color has receded," Sam said, disappointed. "Did it get this far? Tell me it did."

"Yes."

Lila breathed the word, her embarrassment fading faster than her blushes. Sam's touch sent sparks flying through her body. The blood rushed from the surface of her skin, moving like molten lava through her veins. She felt an insistent throb between her legs

"Mmm." Sam licked his lips. "I'm sorry I missed that."

"It's splotchy, not sexy."

"You should let me be the judge of sexy, Lila." Sam's kiss left them both breathless. "Remember, I'm the expert."

Remember? Lila was close to forgetting her own name. Sam kissed her again, his lips firm, commanding. She let him take charge, lead her into a sensual world she knew existed but thought she would never be allowed to enter. Sam was the key. He threw open the door. No. More like smashed it to bits. With his battering ram.

Lila giggled. Battering ram. Where had that come from?

"I like that sound. Want to share?"

"I thought of another penis euphemism."

When she told him, Sam laughed so hard he fell back on the mattress, taking Lila with him. He rolled until she was on top, her lovely breasts pressing into his chest. His hands cupped her butt, aligning her just so, and then sat up. Lila's legs automatically circled his hips. The position was perfect.

"My *battering ram* can feel your…What should we call it?"

"Honeypot?"

"Stop," Sam said, laughing uncontrollably. "All this hilarity is causing friction. It feels amazing. Too amazing. I don't want to embarrass myself all over your stomach."

"If that really is a possibility."

"Considering I've been on edge from the moment I met you? Oh, yeah." Sam leaned back. "Now you're blushing again."

"It's a curse."

"I can see how it would be annoying," Sam conceded. "It makes me want to kiss every inch of your pinkening skin. Follow the path as it spreads up and down your luscious body. Then follow back as it slowly fades. I'm going to find ways to make you blush just so I can enjoy the journey."

"Thank you," Lila said softly. She gave Sam the gentlest of kisses.

"I'm serious."

"I know." This time her kiss was deeper. "Thank you."

They stayed that way, looking deep into each other's eyes. Something passed between them in those moments. Deeper than mere attraction. Stronger than lust.

"I want you. Inside me." Lila whispered the words against his mouth. "Can you reach the table by the bed? In the drawer?"

Keeping one arm firmly around her waist, Sam blindly searched. His hand hit the drawer handle, and then he rummaged around inside. When his fingers brushed a familiar foil packet, he smiled against her lips.

"Are you sure this is my size?"

Lila looked at the package, then swiveled her hips, measuring.

"I'll admit when I bought those yesterday, I was using a bit of wishful thinking." She moved again, smiling. "I'd say I was right on the money. Lucky me."

"Size does matter?" Sam asked, expertly rolling on the condom.

"The user matters," Lila qualified, reaching for him — measuring. "Size is a bonus."

"How do you know…?" Sam swallowed. Lila's hand was making pre-coital teasing banter more and more difficult. "You seem certain I know what I'm doing."

"Reputation." Lila breath hissed between her teeth. Sam's magic fingers were probing between her legs. "You have a good one. Rose confirmed."

Wet, Sam thought with satisfaction. He ran two fingers along her opening. Wet and ready.

"How would Rose know?"

"What?" Her brain was turning to mush. "Stop talking, start —"

Lila almost jumped off the bed, Sam's strong arm around her waist the only thing keeping her mattress-bound. What was he doing? Magic fingers? More like unreal. Beyond talented.

"Tell me what Rose said."

"Now?"

"I could stop."

"No!" Was he kidding? "Inside me, please. Then I promise. I will tell you whatever you want to know."

Sounded like a win-win to him. Sam gripped the sides of Lila's hips, lifting her.

"Take my cock. That's right. You know the rest."

Sam took a deep, calming breath. It took an eternity for Lila to position him. He couldn't tell if she was deliberately torturing him or just a little inexperienced at the process. The look of deep concentration on her face made him think the latter. Okay, he could do this. Let her take her time.

His brain searched for the most unpleasant things possible. Anything to keep his mind off her hand on his dick. Let's see. Landfills, curdled milk, Donald Trump. That helped.

"There," Lila said triumphantly.

"Perfect, honey. Take me at your own pace. Don't rush. Slow, easy."

Buoyed by his soft, encouraging tone, Lila used Sam's shoulders to steady herself. The feeling of being in control smoothed out the rest of her nerves. This was what she needed, where she wanted to be. Following his advice, she took him in a bit at a time. Part of her wanted to hurry, get to the good part. Her body knew this was good. Why rush through something that felt close to heaven? She planned on getting there; first, she wanted to savor the journey.

"There," Sam sighed with relief. It hadn't been easy; he gritted his teeth the entire time. Lila's look of accomplishment made it worth it.

"Should I move?"

Sam lifted both hands, cupping her head. His kiss was thorough, letting her know with his tongue what he would soon be doing with his cock.

"Soon."

Sam laughed at her look of frustration. *Trust me*, he wanted to assure her. *I know how you feel.* It was tempting to grab her hips, thrust himself up again. To end this. To fill the aching need he knew was shared by them both. For some reason, he wanted it to last as long as possible. It didn't matter that they had all night. He could take her again and again. This was the first time. Four, five, six more times. What he did *this* time more than any other was how she would remember him. He planned to make it something no other man would ever be able to equal.

"Tell me about your conversation with Rose."

"It would serve you right if I refused."

"Then we both would lose."

Sam cupped her breasts, sighing with happiness. A soft, firm, perfect handful. He rubbed her nipples with his thumbs, causing her to squirm, lifting slightly, and then coming down again on his rock hard erection.

"Careful," he warned, taking a nipple into his mouth. He bit causing her to jump with surprise, not pain.

"Like that?"

"You know I do."

"Then tell me what Rose said and I'll do it again."

Lila growled with frustration. She could tell he was serious. He wanted to talk about Rose while they were... He wanted to talk about Rose.

"Are you hung up on her?"

Sam was busy watching his hands on Lila's breasts. The weight, the way her nipple felt on his palms when he ran them over the hard bud. How dark his tanned skin looked next to the milky whiteness of hers.

"Who? Rose? Why on earth would you think that?"

"You seem awfully interested in what she had to say about you."

Sam's hips thrust up, ever so slightly.

"Don't," Lila moaned. "Not until you answer."

"Rose is getting an awful lot of play."

"My thoughts exactly."

"Fine."

Sam kept his hands on her breasts but raised his eyes to hers. A lot wary, a little turned on. Time to cut the wary altogether. The turned on would grow from there.

"Rose is a beautiful, desirable woman. I invited her to my bed on several occasions. She turned me down flat every time." He kept his gaze steady, easy to read. "I wasn't offended or obsessed. I like her. I'm curious to know if she talked me up or warned you to steer clear."

Believing him, Lila relaxed and smiled.

"Both. The warning came first. When she realized I couldn't be dissuaded, she confirmed the rumors."

"Which are?"

"Come on, Sam. You know what women say about you. Great in bed, generous. Guaranteed orgasms."

Sam was about to say more when Lila moved again. The rest of the conversation could wait. She was expecting an orgasm? It was past time he delivered.

He moved his hands to her hips, his mouth latching onto one of those oh so tempting breasts.

"Sam," Lila cried out, half pleasure, half protest. "I wanted to know about your reputation."

"Time for show, not tell, Lila."

There it was, Sam thought. Her eyes turned liquid gold. Close. They both were. Too much time teasing and talking. He urged her to meet his hips with hers.

"Come with me, Lila."

Sam reached between them, finding the spot that would send her over. There. He heard the change in her breathing, felt her muscles clench around him. Throwing his head back, he shouted her name. A second later, she joined him, his name on her lips.

Movements slowing, milking the last bit of sensation for them both, Sam kissed Lila. Long, slow. The desperation over, he gave her tenderness, holding her close when she collapsed into his arms.

Sam ran a soothing hand up and down Lila's back. How many times had he held a woman just like this? Waited as their heartbeat slowed back to normal? More than he would count. The pleasure blurred as did the faces.

That was how Sam knew. This was different. Lila was different. When he left her bed, she wouldn't become one of many. He'd wanted to make sure she remembered. Now he was caught in a trap of his own making. Not only would he never forget Lila Fleming, he didn't want to.

"YOU SHOULD HAVE told me."

"I wouldn't be telling you now if you hadn't gone all crazy protective brother the second Lila didn't answer her phone."

"Do I have to remind you of all the shit that's gone down lately?" Alex asked. He tried to keep his voice down to a low roar. He wasn't succeeding.

"Of course not."

"Then how is it overreacting when my sister is AWOL?"

"Listen to yourself," Dani said. "This isn't the Army and your sister isn't one of your wayward recruits. She's a grown woman who has the right to a little privacy."

"With that, that…" Alex searched for the perfect word. "Reprobate?"

"Good word," Dani admitted, and then got back to the argument. "She's fine. Lila has spent the night with other men. I don't recall you threatening bodily harm to them."

"That's because I didn't know about it until after the fact." Alex looked at the clock by their bed. "One in the morning. As we speak, they might be," Alex swallowed, "you know."

"I tell you what."

Dani reached over, taking his phone from his tense fingers. She dropped it into the drawer on her side of the bed.

"Instead of worrying about Lila, why don't you show me what people do at this time of the night?"

She kissed him, her hand slipping under the covers.

"Very nice," she said, feeling the length of his growing erection.

"I'm going over there first thing in the morning."

"Mmm," Dani placated with several more kisses. "Maybe wait until ten."

Alex moved his head to the side, giving Dani better access.

"Nine."

Dani smiled. Lifting the covers, she paused, her mouth inches from taking him inside. One swipe of her tongue, his accompanying moan, and she knew she had him. Lila's privacy was safe from her brother's protective prying. And she was in for a very pleasurable night.

Chapter Four

LILA WHISTLED HER way through her morning work. She was happy. Giddy. And why not? Hours of sexual bliss in the arms of a man who looked like he stepped off the cover of GQ was funny, kind, sweet. There were almost as many laughs as orgasms. And a few tears. They exchanged growing up stories. Telling Sam about the death of her parents was difficult yet surprisingly cathartic. She didn't talk about that time to many people. Her brother — Dani. Rose, and Tyler knew. A close circle of friends. Now Sam.

Lila cried a little. Then he asked her about the good times. No one did that. They always expressed sympathy then moved on from the difficult subject. Sam gave her a chance to remember her parents in the best possible way. Happy — alive. A weight she hadn't been aware of lifted. She felt lighter. Sam gave her that. She gave him another piece of her heart.

Sam proved to be full of all kinds of surprises. He woke her with his mouth. Oral sex had always been a mystery to Lila. She didn't like giving; she never got any pleasure receiving. Until now.

At first, Lila thought she was having the hottest sex dream ever. Sam, doing wicked things to her with his mouth. For the first time, she enjoyed having a man down there. No embarrassment, no awkward tap on the head saying nice try, no cigar. This time, everything was working. His tongue and fingers were in perfect sync, bringing her immeasurable pleasure.

"I'm dreaming," she moaned.

"Me too," a voice answered. "Only in a dream could a woman be so pretty *and* taste like nectar from the gods."

Lila's eyes popped open, a gasp on her lips. *Not a dream.* Sam was... Holy crap. She tried to sit up, move away. The lack of embarrassment her dream provided came rushing in, full force.

"Sam, you have to stop."

"I will," he said, holding her hips steady so she couldn't get away. "Give me another five, ten minutes and I promise to stop."

"But..." Lila moaned, louder than in her dream. Or non-dream. "I don't like that. I mean, I've never gotten any pleasure...What are you doing?"

"Enjoying my pre-breakfast snack."

Lila was too far gone to protest. She laid down, shutting off her mind. The fingers spread through his thick, soft hair, pulling him closer, urging him on. It didn't take even close to five minutes for her to reach that elusive oral sex peak.

When Lila finally became aware of her surroundings, she slowly opened her eyes.

"Sam."

"Mmm."

"Why are you still down there?" She tried to close her legs without any success. Sam's shoulders made it impossible.

"I like the view." His bright blue eyes traveled up her body then back down again. "Beautiful. Too many men don't take the time to enjoy every angle of a woman's body."

"You've seen it all before."

"Every woman is different, Lila," Sam explained, his hand sliding up her stomach over her ribs until he cupped her breast.

"Not *that* different."

"Wrong. The differences are infinite."

Sam scooted up, taking her in his arms.

"Do you know what it takes to be a good lover?"

"Amazing hands, fantastic cock, and talented tongue?"

"No," Sam chuckled. "Though that all helps. Technique is great, I'm all for it."

"Love the technique, big fan."

"Smartass."

"Hey, I'm serious."

"Then let me enlighten you, Grasshopper." Sam laced his fingers with Lila's. He liked the connection. "The secret, after learning the basics, is caring about your partner. When I'm with a woman, my pleasure is magnified when she is enjoying it as much as I am."

"That myth is smashed to bits."

"What myth?"

"The one that says good looking men are often terrible lovers because they don't have to try. Women fall at their feet." Lila cupped Sam's face giving him a long, deep kiss. "You aren't supposed to care if I have fun, as long as you do."

"I thought we established my well-earned reputation as an orgasm machine," Sam joked.

"True," Lila conceded, her eyes twinkling. "You can be the exception to the rule."

"Unique?"

"You like that?"

Sam turned his head and shrugged.

"I've never wanted to be one among many." Sam turned, pushing Lila onto her back. "In the bedroom, my motto is quality *and* quantity."

"Nope."

Lila pushed back. She knew Sam let her, happy to allow her to spread her wings a little and take control.

This time it was Lila who gave Sam's body a long, appreciative once over.

"Well?"

"You'll do."

The truth was Lila didn't know how she wound up in bed with the hottest man on the planet. Not one to look a gift horse in the mouth, she decided not to worry about it — just enjoy.

Part of the fun was finding out she wasn't as vanilla in bed as she always thought. Man on top, woman on bottom. *Boring.* Suddenly, in one night she found herself doing things, having things done to her, she only read about in books. Giving a man a blowjob might not be blindingly original. Or new. But this time, like when he went down on her, she planned to enjoy it.

"Grab the headboard, Sam. I'm about to *blow* your mind."

Now, Lila checked her watch, two short hours later, she could officially say blowjobs were awesome. With the right man.

Lila felt her happiness wane, just a bit. Sam. He was the right man. The man who would walk out of her life today. When she told her friends that her heart couldn't be broken in one day, Lila was right. Not broken — just severely cracked.

"I told you, the cyber campaign needs to be pushed out before the first of the year. I don't care if you're visiting your family. That's why we have computers. Get your ass in gear or you won't have a job to come back to."

Lila's eyes widened. Whomever Sam was talking to, was getting a royal reaming out. If they weren't shaking in their boots, they weren't human.

The mostly one-sided conversation continued in the same vein for several more minutes. Sam's voice getting louder, his language increasingly colorful.

"Hi."

Sam came down the stairs, his hair still damp from his shower. The smile on his face, open, affectionate, showed a completely different man than the one she overheard. This was the Sam she welcomed to her bed. Deep down, Lila knew they were one and the same. That made him what? *An intimate stranger?* A disconcerting thought.

"Is something wrong?"

Sam crossed the room, his arms wrapping around her waist. He gave her the sweetest kiss. *Okay*, she thought, *back to Dr. Jekyll. He must have left Mr. Hyde upstairs.*

"No."

"Yes." Sam tipped her chin up, his eyes concerned. "You look worried."

"You aren't really going to fire that poor person, are you?"

"What person?" Sam frowned. He looked up at the staircase, the light dawning. "You heard that."

"I think all of Harper Falls heard that. You were very... vocal."

"Business."

"*Business*? Is that usual?" she asked warily. "I would hesitate to do business with anyone who talked to me like that."

"I wouldn't blame you." Sam sighed, briefly resting his forehead on hers. When he straightened, his expression was rueful.

"I was talking to Malcolm, my assistant in New York. He had clear, concise instructions. Things that needed to be done before he left for his Christmas holiday."

"I take it Malcolm screwed up."

"He did. I'm in a very fickle business, Lila. What's hot this week is easily forgotten the next. If I say something needs doing, it doesn't mean next week; it meant yesterday."

"*Are* you going to fire him?"

"Not this time." Sighing, Sam pulled her in tight, his hands giving her back a soothing rub. "Contrary to what some might tell you, I'm not unreasonable. I hold my employees up to the same standards I expect from myself. If they're just learning, like Malcolm, they get some slack."

"Just enough to hang themselves?"

"Smartass," Sam chuckled. "No, enough to learn. Malcolm is on strike two. He's been with me for almost a year, Lila. He knows how I work. He's watched me fire people who wouldn't get with the program."

Lila pushed out of Sam's embrace. He couldn't read her expression. Was she that upset by what she had overheard?

"Lila, like I said, it's business. I have no problem shutting it off the rest of the time."

"I know," Lila assured him. "I'm embarrassed."

"Why?"

"Because *your* business is none of mine." She shrugged. "I was startled by what I heard, that's all. I wasn't thinking. I remember Rose once telling me that you could be a trifle... intense about your work."

"Did she?"

Sam smiled. A *trifle* intense? He remembered being a damn hard-ass. He pushed Rose, never letting up. It was his way; he didn't know any other. She wasn't intimidated. She didn't blink. In fact, she gave as good as she got. Turned out to be one of the best experiences of his professional life.

"It doesn't matter, Sam."

"But..."

"Honestly." Lila kissed his cheek, then lingered on his mouth. "You're leaving in a few hours. Let's not talk about your work."

"About that."

"Your work?"

"No," Sam said. He took a deep breath, suddenly less sure. "I want to stay. The rest of the week."

"You do?"

Sam understood the surprise he saw on Lila's face. He felt the same. He took his shower, mentally going over his schedule. Los Angeles for the next few days, a stopover in New York. Paris in time for the New Year. Then he thought of Lila. What would she be doing at midnight on the thirty-first? Who would she be with? Who would she kiss as the clock struck twelve?

It didn't take long for him to figure that one out. She should kiss him.

Why not? He could rearrange meetings. His plans for New Year's Eve were tentative. Several invitations, nothing set in stone.

As Sam rinsed Lila's shampoo from his hair, the scent of her filling the room, he made up his mind. Until now, he hadn't thought about Lila's reaction. Maybe she wouldn't want him to stay. One night might be all she wanted.

"I don't want to push myself on you, Lila. I want to stay; if you'll have me."

Lila didn't know what to say. She left her bed this morning prepared to say goodbye. Resigned. Sam was never meant to be more than one wonderful night. A memory to savor. Suddenly, he offered her a few more days.

Her first impulse was to shout, *YES!* She would take as much of him as she could get. As she opened her mouth to do just that, the words wouldn't come out. By nature, Lila was not an impulsive person. She thought things through. The longer she thought, the more she knew this was a bad idea.

Her heart was already hovering between like and love. Another week with Sam was bound to cement her firmly on the side of love. If she let him walk away now, no harm done. A tinge of regret, that's all. If he stayed, she faced a broken heart for the New Year.

Tell him no, her rational side urged. *No, no, no, no, no.*

Lila looked up at Sam. Sweet, sexy, complicated Sam. In the end, there was only one thing she could say.

"Yes."

"YOU SAID HE was leaving today."

"That's what I understood, Alex." Dani exchanged eye rolls with Rose. "I'm not responsible for Sam Laughton changing his plans."

"One night," Alex grumbled. He gave Jack an accusatory look. "What is it with one-night stands? No one honors them anymore?"

"If you're referring to my one-night stand with Rose —"

"Exactly," Alex exclaimed. "She asked for something very specific. One night, no strings attached. Simple. Traditional. Jack screwed all that up by refusing to give her what she wanted."

"Traditional?" Rose almost choked on her sweet roll. "What is traditional about non-committal sex? And may I remind you, he did give me what I wanted — eventually. My one-night stand turned into forever." She laid her hand on Jack's, the ring he placed there shining bright. "No complaints here."

"Sam Laughton isn't sticking around Harper Falls. No happily ever after for Lila."

The friends were meeting for a post-Christmas breakfast at Harper Falls newest eatery. *Let Them Eat Croissants* followed in the footsteps of other businesses in town. The cuter and punnier, the better. This French patisserie was sandwiched between *Eye Saw You Coming,* an optometrist and *Take Me Out To The Ball Gown,* a shop specializing in formal wear.

Alex was five minutes into his rant, the hot coffee in front of him going cold, his chocolate croissant forgotten. Jack, believing in waste not want not, snatched the roll from his friend's plate, taking a hearty bite.

"There is an age-old covenant," Alex grumbled. "One night means one night."

"Where is that written?" Drew asked. He slapped Tyler's hand when she tried purloining his coffee. "Patience, Ty. The waitress is making the rounds. You can wait thirty seconds for a refill."

Tyler wasn't sure. She needed her morning caffeine. One cup, delicious as it was, didn't cut it. She gave Drew her sweetest *please* smile.

"Fine," Drew sighed. What could he do? He loved this woman. Feeding her addiction came with the territory. He pushed his cup in front of her. His reward? A big, enthusiastic kiss. Who needed coffee? Tyler was enough to jump-start *his* day.

"What is wrong with all of you," Alex demanded. "My sister is in the clutches of a world-famous letch. You're calmly eating pastry and arguing over coffee."

"First," Rose said reasonably. "No one is arguing. Jack *stole* your roll. Drew *gave* Tyler his coffee. Second," she continued before Alex exploded again, "Sam Laughton is not a letch. He likes women. Treats them with respect."

"But —"

"Anything," she continued, "that is going on between him and Lila, is one hundred percent consensual."

"She's right, Alex."

Dani squeezed his hand. She understood why he was worried. All the years Alex was in the Army, he did his part to keep this country safe. It was an important job; one he was good at. Keeping his sister safe wasn't possible. For the first time in ten years, the siblings lived in the same town. Overprotective brother mode came naturally. It was up to Dani and his friends to help him dial it back several notches.

"Lila should be here, with us. Now." Alex looked around the table. "Do you know why she isn't?"

"Because her brother is a pain in her ass she'd rather not deal with?" Jack suggested not so innocently.

Alex gave his old friend a dirty look.

"She's with that, that… *movie producer.*"

"I doubt he has her chained to the radiator."

"Really?" Dani turned to Drew. "Why did you have to put that image in his head?"

"That's it." Alex took out his phone. "What's his number?"

Deciding a phone call was better than rushing over to Lila's, Rose pulled up the number on her phone, hitting dial before handing it to Alex.

"What are you going to do?" Dani asked her fiancé warily. When he didn't answer right away, she laid a hand on his arm. "Do not embarrass Lila."

"Don't worry," Alex reassured the love of his life. Unfortunately, his cold, steel smile negated his words. "I'm just going to invite him for a friendly drink."

"At *Tom Tom's?*" Jack asked with a grin.

"At *Tom Tom's.*"

Chapter Five

TOM TOM'S WAS a Harper Falls institution. Opened by a first Gulf War vet, it was considered a rite of passage to have your first legal drink there. If you were underage, you better not sneak in. Tom Unger had a nose for sniffing out a fake I.D. Once caught, you weren't allowed back in, legal or not. Everyone knew the rule. Those who tried to get around it paid the price.

Once a month Tom closed early. Other vets from the area gathered to play poker, air out their personal problems, or simply hang with people who had seen the same kind of hell and lived to talk about it. This was one of those nights.

Sam didn't know any of this when he agreed to have a drink with Lila's brother. That he was going at all, didn't sit well with the lady.

"You don't have to do this," Lila told him after he got off the phone with Alex. "He's treating me like a Victorian virgin. You can't deflower or debauch me."

"No debauching? I'm sorry to hear that."

"Besides," Lila continued, not buying into Sam's attempt at humor, "we only have a few days. This is my time."

"We'll have all night," Sam assured her. "One drink. Two at the most. I charm your brother; assure him I'm as tame as a pussycat. Once

I calm his fears, we can enjoy the rest of the week."

"You don't know my brother," Lila told him. "He's a hard-ass when it comes to protecting the women in his life. He sees me as the same girl I was when he left home to join the Army. I've tried. Dani's tried. Nothing can break through that thick skull."

"I can testify; you are all woman."

"Whatever you do, don't even hint that you've seen me naked."

Sam put his arms around her, pulling her close.

"If push comes to shove, I can take care of myself," Sam assured her. "I trained with an expert in Krav Maga."

Between them, Alex, Jack, and Drew were over six-hundred pounds of solid muscle. Lila knew if there were a fight, it would be one on one. Alex wouldn't bring his friends into it. Unfortunately for Sam, Alex alone would be more than enough.

No matter how much *training* Sam had, her brother's experience was garnered out in the field. The desert of Kuwait, the mountains of Afghanistan. She didn't want to hurt his male ego, so she kept quiet. But if push came to shove, Sam would be pushed and shoved into the hospital.

"I can't talk you out of this?"

"Lila." Sam kissed the end of her nose. "Drinks at a local bar. What's the worst that could happen?"

SAM WATCHED AS the lights of Harper Falls faded behind them. *What was the worst that could happen?* Three large men could kill him, dispose of the body, and use each other as alibis. Maybe Lila was right. This was not a good idea.

"Where *is* this place?" he asked Alex. When Lila's brother didn't answer, he turned to the men in the back of the SUV. "I thought Tom Tom's was in Harper Falls."

"Technically, it's outside the city limits," Jack told him. The usually smiling man's face wore an unusually stern expression.

"Sit back," Drew said. "We're almost there."

Ten minutes ago, getting in the big, black SUV seemed like the logical thing to do. No point in taking two rigs, Alex told him.

While Sam greeted Jack and Drew, Lila took Alex aside. He couldn't hear the heated conversation; he could tell it was mostly one sided — Lila's side. She was animated, gesturing, her finger pointing. All the while, Alex stood silently, arms crossed over his massive chest. When Lila finally wound down, without a word, Alex gently patted his sister's shoulder, then kissed her cheek.

"Damn it, Alex," Lila called out as they left the shop. "Behave yourself."

Thinking of that moment, Sam wondered if the little, unconcerned wave he gave Lila as the door closed behind him, was the last time he would see her. It was silly. Alex and his friends were not going to kill him. Beat him up? That was possible. He could take a punch from a normal man. Unfortunately, these guys, with their training, experience, and size, were anything but normal. His big words to Lila about Krav Maga were said to alleviate her worry. He knew he was no match for these men. Unlike Lila, he hadn't realized he would need to be.

"Here we are," Jack called out.

Whatever Sam expected, it wasn't this.

The parking lot of the long, dark green building was empty; a single light over the door cast an almost eerie glow. Not the most welcoming sight.

"Is the place open?"

"Yes and no," Alex said as he put the SUV in park.

Sam slowly unbuckled his seat belt. The other three men were already out of the vehicle, waiting for Sam to join them. He'd asked for this, no backing out now. With a resigned sigh, Sam reached for the door handle.

The cold night air hit his face, bracing after the heated SUV. Jack slapped him on the back.

"Don't look so glum. You aren't going to your execution."

"Is that a promise?"

Jack looked at Alex, then shrugged. "I can almost guarantee it. Damn, it's colder than a witch's tit. Let's get inside."

"I SHOULD HAVE kept my mouth shut," Lila said. She paced the length of her apartment, then turned. The three women and two dogs watched, back and forth, back and forth. Like they were witnessing a one-sided tennis match.

"What were you going to do?" Dani asked. "Hole up here for the entire week? Alex was bound to find out Sam hadn't left town. More than shit would have hit the fan after that."

Lila stopped, her fists clenched in frustration. "Why is it any of his business?"

"That was my question," Tyler said. "It got me a very dirty look."

"Of course, Jack and Drew had to jump in and be all, *we men have to protect our women*." Rose shook her head. "I think they just wanted to be there to cheer Alex on in case a fight breaks out."

"What?"

"Nice going," Dani said to Rose. "Lila, calm down. Do not grab your keys."

"I need to get to Tom Tom's."

Lila headed for the door, and then remembered it was winter. Before she could backtrack to her closet, Dani calmly took the car keys from her hand and led her to the sofa.

"Sit."

"But…"

"Listen," Dani settled her friend. Pouring a glass of wine, she handed it to Lila. "Nothing is going to happen. I made Alex promise he would deliver Sam back to you in the same condition he was in when he left."

"No black eyes? No missing teeth? Sam has great teeth," Lila told the other women. "No caps or veneers. He was born with them."

"I'd be more worried about his balls than his teeth."

"Really?" Dani exclaimed. She turned to Rose. "What is with you tonight? I'm trying to put out a fire. You're trailing behind with a can of gasoline."

"Sorry," Rose said. She grasped Lila's hand. "Dani's right. Alex isn't a hot head. Jack is a born peacemaker. Drew is the wild card. You never can tell what he might do."

"Hey," Tyler exclaimed. "No need to throw my man under the bus." Thinking for a moment, she backtracked. "Okay, I'll give you that one. Drew can be unpredictable, which I love. But he has no reason to go after Sam, or egg Alex on."

"See?" Dani said, patting Lila's hand reassuringly. "Sam will be fine."

As if sensing her distress, Cooper padded over. He put his head on Lila's knee, eager to comfort.

"You understand, don't you?"

Lila put her arms around his neck, burrowing her face into the fur. The big dog seemed to understand they were talking about Sam.

You fell in love him right away, didn't you, boy?

Cooper's big brown eyes seemed to say, *"You, too."*

Me? No. Lila sighed. *But I'm falling. Hard and fast.*

"I'LL SEE YOUR dollar and raise you two more."

"Somebody's feeling lucky."

"Luck has nothing to do with it. Skill, my friend, nothing but skill."

Sam grinned. The two men exchanging words did so with little heat and obvious affection. Old friends, easy camaraderie. The entire group felt like a laid-back social circle. He had to remind himself these guys met for a reason other than poker. They were a support group. Vets helping vets. He didn't belong. Normally, he would feel out of place. An intruder. Tonight was an exception. They allowed him, Jack, and Drew in because one of their own requested it.

"You're awfully quiet, Sam. I thought you show business types talked all the time."

Sam looked at Tom Unger. He owned *Tom Tom's,* was the group's unofficial leader. It was obvious they looked to him, followed his rules — happily. Be respectful; don't drink too much. Screw up one time too many, don't come back.

"Oh, I can talk your ear off if the situation warrants it," Sam said. He took a sip of beer. "I'm still wondering if I'm here for a talking to or an ass whipping."

"The ass whipping is up to Alex." Tom chuckled. "Don't look so worried. He's a reasonable sort — most of the time. Mess with a man's sister, reason tends to fly out the window."

"I'm not messing with —"

"We're all fond of Lila," Tom interrupted. "She's like one of my own."

Hearing this, the other men at the table chimed in. Lila was either a sister, a daughter, a friend. Steve, new to the group and younger than the rest, let everyone know she was hot. The comment earned him some warning looks and an elbow to the ribs. From Sam.

"Hey," Steve complained. "I didn't say I would ever do anything about it. Isn't a guy allowed to look?"

"Absolutely," Tom told him. "Look, enjoy. Keep your mouth shut. Understood?"

"Understood, Tom."

Impressive. A few softly spoken words, direct eye contact. Tom had the respect of these men. It was genuine, and, if Sam wasn't mistaken, mutual.

"If you ever want a job as my assistant director, let me know. You'd keep everyone in line with a single look."

"I'll keep the offer in mind," Tom said. "Now, let's get down to why you're here tonight."

"Finally," Alex exclaimed. Tom deliberately put the two men on opposite sides of the table. In theory, great. Sam could have done without an evening of dirty looks.

"Alex." Tom's voice was firm. "When you called me to set this up, you agreed to let us take Sam's measure before anything was said or done."

"We've been here two hours, Tom," Alex pointed out. "I've known you to *take a man's measure* in thirty seconds. What's the holdup?"

Unoffended by Alex's outburst, Tom shrugged. "I've made up my mind about Sam. Didn't take long."

"Then —"

Tom held up a hand, instantly silencing Alex.

"I didn't want to influence anyone. You and Lila are family, son."

Sam saw Alex swallow hard when Tom called him son. It seemed the older man was more than a friend; he was a surrogate father. Suddenly this all made sense. If Alex's father were alive, he would consult him. Now, that was Tom's job.

"Sam is a good man," Tom told them. "A little arrogant. Too used to getting his own way," he looked at Alex. "Sound familiar? You met your lady in another country. Her brother was here, blissfully unaware of what was happening."

"I respected Dani," Alex said, a bit defensively.

"I respect Lila." Sam directed his words to Tom. His glanced at Alex, wanting him to understand. "I'll admit this get-together threw me. I've never had a brother, or any family member, worry about a woman I was seeing. Lila is very lucky to have all of you in her life."

"Well said, Sam." Tom looked around the table. Each man nodded. When his eyes stopped on Alex, everyone grew quiet.

"She's my sister," Alex grumbled. There was less heat, more resignation. "Don't hurt her."

"I would rather cut off my left nut."

"Hurt her," Alex told him, "I'll do it for you."

"FINALLY." LILA JUMPED up when she heard the door to the shop open. "I thought they would never get back."

"Four hours," Dani reminded her. "That's about average for poker night."

"Seemed like an eternity."

Lila stopped herself from racing down the stairs. The slightly sick feeling in her stomach grew. The sound of feet on the stairs, more than one pair. One more second, she would scream.

Alex was the first one into the room.

"Don't give me that look," he said. "Loverboy is still in one piece. See?"

Sam looked fine. No visible marks. She started to go to him but her brother's hand on her arm stopped her.

"Nope." He pulled her close, giving her a loving hug. "Big brother first." Alex kissed her cheek, and then whispered, "He was never in any danger."

"I know," she whispered back. Her arms tightened around his waist. She loved him so much. "I was afraid you might stick him on one of Jack and Drew's planes, and then have one of them fly him out of here. Maybe Timbuktu or Kathmandu."

"Mmm, it was a thought." Alex laughed when Lila punched him in the arm. "He's here, isn't he? No harm done."

"Was there any?" Lila asked Sam after everyone left. "Harm done, I mean."

"I'm good. Perfect."

"You've come out of this with your ego intact," Lila laughed. "What went on tonight?"

"Guy stuff," Sam said. He removed his coat and gloves before bending to pet a wiggling Cooper.

"Guy stuff? What? Spitting and cursing and peeing standing up?"

"Pissing."

"I beg your pardon?"

"Guys say piss, not pee." Sam took her in his arms, his grin wide.

"I hate that word; it's… crude."

"My point exactly." He kissed a trail along her jaw. "Men *are* crude. Get a group of us together, and it flows like water. Raunchy jokes. Some bragging over sexual exploits. *Past* sexual exploits. No mention was made of any current relationships."

Lila shook her head in amazement. "Men. Why do you think women are different? We cuss. We tell inappropriate jokes. As for bragging? You wouldn't believe some of the stories I've heard."

"Fair enough." Sam lifted Lila, his arms strong and sure. He headed for the bedroom. "What do you say we give a few more to add to your arsenal?"

Lila didn't tell Sam. Before him, she had no stories. None interesting enough to brag over. By the end of the week, she would. Envy-inducing tales. Lila knew one thing. She would keep the good parts to herself.

These moments were *hers*. For the next few days, Sam belonged to her. She wasn't going to share. Not now. Not ever.

SAM QUIETLY LEFT the bed. Watching Lila sleep was a joy. When her eyes were open, she was a constant bundle of beautiful energy. Relaxed, her breathing gentle, she was just as beautiful. This was different. Peaceful. She made his heart —

No. Sam put a screeching halt to those thoughts. His heart was not involved. It couldn't be. Lila belonged in Harper Falls. She had her brother, her friends. He needed the rest of the world. He needed excitement. He craved big cities. New York, London, Los Angeles. His home in Paris. As lovely as Harper Falls was, he knew it wasn't for him. All he had to offer Lila was the occasional visit. She deserved more. She deserved it all. A husband. Children. He wanted all those things too. Someday. But not here. She was planting roots and they were getting deeper every day. Any future for them was impossible.

"Hey, Coop."

Cooper greeted him with a happy smile, his head tipped to the side. Sam would miss him. It hadn't taken long for the dog to worm his way into Sam's affections. A bit like a certain curvy brunette.

"I'm in trouble, Coop," Sam confided to his furry friend. "Promise you'll look after her. I expect you to be a gentleman, keep her company. Keep her safe. Especially keep her safe."

Sam poured himself a glass of water, then filled Cooper's bowl. The sound of the dog lapping up water followed him as he wandered around the room. It was a small living area. Probably too small now that a large dog was added to the mix. They would make do. When she found the right man, they would move to a bigger place.

Sam frowned at the thought. He wasn't that man, but picturing Lila with anyone else made his stomach clench. God, he was a selfish bastard. Not that it was a revelation. He was used to having his way — getting what he wanted. He wanted Lila. Couldn't have her. What did he expect? Lila wasn't going into hiding when he left town. Some lucky bastard would snatch her up. He hoped he never heard when it happened.

Lila's desk was neat, like the rest of her apartment. A cordless phone, a laptop. In one corner a spiral notebook with a plain white cover sat. Curious, Sam sat in the chair. He knew this was snooping. The book was closed. That didn't stop him longer than a few seconds. If she wanted to keep the contents private, the drawer was less than a foot away. His reasoning was slightly skewed, but it worked for him. Flipping open the cover, Sam began to read.

Lila stretched her arms above her head. Mmm. The bed was warm, perfect for a cuddle with a big sexy man. To her disappointment, when she reached for Sam, his side was empty. She felt the around. Empty and cold.

Certain he wouldn't have left without telling her, Lila grabbed her robe. The apartment was silent, but there was a faint beam of light under the door. Lila stepped out of the bedroom, searching. When she saw Sam sitting at her desk, reading from her notebook, she started forward. His laughter stopped her in her tracks.

"Which part are you reading?"

Sam's head whipped around, startled.

"Lila," he began. It was too late to feign guilt. It wasn't too late to apologize. "I'm sorry, honey. I know I should have asked first."

"Yes, you should have." She tightened the belt on her robe, and then crossed to join him. "You find my story funny?"

"Funny, sweet, moving. I planned on glancing at it, nothing more. One paragraph and I couldn't put it down."

"I…" she tried to find the words. "Sometimes it's easier to write what I'm feeling."

Sam went to her, clasping her hand in his. So small and delicate. Like Lila. And like the woman, strong — capable. He gently kissed her cheek.

"The girl in the story. Did you know her?"

"Yes." Lila laid her head on Sam's chest. The beat of his heart both comforting and stirring. "I had a friend in Oregon — my best friend. She lived next door. When she got sick, the cancer moved so fast. I never said goodbye. After all these years, with this story, I'm finally getting to..."

Sam led Lila to the sofa, sitting. He tucked her close, his arm around her.

"The part before, when the girls spy on the brother kissing his girlfriend?"

"That was me," she chuckled.

"The description was priceless. The friend intrigued because of her crush on the older boy. The sister. You. Embarrassed."

"I really made you laugh? You aren't just saying that?"

"You heard me." Sam gave her a straight, clear look. "I didn't know you were there, Lila. But I promise if I had, I wouldn't have laughed to make you feel good."

Lila sighed. "Good. You're the first person to read that story."

"Do you have more?"

"No." Lila shook her head. "Oh, I have some terrible poetry. My angsty teenage phase. In college, I majored in business. My mother encouraged me to take a few creative writing courses. When she died, my desire to write died. Recently, something brought me back to it."

"You're talented, Lila."

Lila's first instinct was to dismiss Sam's compliment. This was her secret, her dream. Having someone feed that dream, especially someone whose opinion she respected, made her uncomfortable. She could hear her mother's encouraging words. The love washed over her. Lila's eyes filled with tears. *Someone else thinks my writing is good, Mom.*

"Hey," Sam said, worry in his eyes. "Why the tears? What I said is a good thing."

"It is," Lila assured him. She hesitated. "Don't laugh."

"Promise."

"I miss my mother."

"Oh, honey." Sam gave her a sweet kiss. "Of course you do."

"She thought I could be a writer, Sam. When you told me I was good, it felt like she was here, wrapping her arms around me. I haven't felt this close to her in years."

Without a word, Sam held her close, letting the gentle tears flow. He felt a tightness in his throat. He couldn't give Lila back her mother. He could help make her dreams come true.

"I know people, Lila."

"We all do, Sam," Lila smiled, her cheeks glistening.

Looking around, Sam found the box of tissues on the coffee table. Grabbing one, he dabbed away her tears.

"*My* people are publishers."

"No."

Lila tried to move away, but Sam held her tight.

"Don't dismiss the idea until you hear me out."

"I don't want my story published."

"But —"

"If I did, I wouldn't want my..." she struggled for the right word. "Whatever you are, using his influence."

"I could get pissed off, fast, at such an accusation." Sam took a deep, calming breath. "You don't know me very well, so let me make something clear. This is my business, Lila. I don't screw around with that. Nepotism, cronyism. I didn't get where I am by putting unqualified, untalented people ahead of more deserving candidates."

"I'm sorry," Lila said, ashamed of herself. "I don't think of myself as a professional writer. It's hard to wrap my head around the idea of being *that* good."

"Well, start."

"This story was never meant to be seen, Sam. Maybe something else. Someday."

"*This*," Sam insisted. "*Now*."

"It's personal," Lila protested. "Who wants to read my ramblings?"

"I do."

"But —"

"Writing about your friend. It's your way of finishing the healing process."

"Yes."

"Think of all the young people dealing with the issue. This story might help." Sam tucked her under his arm, his hand smoothing back her hair. "When *Wishes* came out, the reviews fed my ego. You know what fed my soul? When someone would tell me how much the movie touched them. One lady said she cried for two hours straight then called her mother. They saw it together the next day."

"Did she cry again?"

"They both did," Sam said. "Like babies."

"I don't know, Sam." It was tempting. For so many reasons.

"Think about it. No hurry. No pressure."

"Really?"

Hearing the doubt in her voice, Sam smiled. His reputation for getting what he wanted was well known — and well earned.

"I promise not to push — for now. A month, maybe two, down the road? No guarantees."

Lila felt a rush of emotion that had nothing to with her book. *A month,* maybe *two, down the road.* A chance to have contact with Sam after this week. Did that make her a glutton for punishment? Getting all tingly thinking about a *chance* to talk with Sam at some unsettled date? Lila didn't care. She would take what she could get and worry about the implications later.

"Deal."

Sam pulled Lila in for a long kiss. He wondered if she realized what she had agreed to. As far as he was concerned, she gave him permission to walk back into her life. As he deepened the kiss, his hands delving under her robe, Sam knew one thing. He wouldn't wait long. A month? He could go without seeing her, touching her, for that long. Then Lila moaned. Her fingers threaded through his hair. The kiss escalated, soared.

"Three weeks," Sam hissed through his teeth when her hand left his hair to cup his erection.

"Hmm?" Lila asked. Her eyes were cloudy with passion.

"Nothing, honey."

Sam lifted Lila. Would his arms feel empty after he left her? Two weeks would be pushing his luck. Three. Definitely three.

Chapter Six

THE WEEK FLEW by. Time never dragged when you wanted it to. Lila felt like she was in a strange bubble. Insulated from the outside world, yet aware that as every minute passed, their time together slipped away.

With the holiday rush behind her, she could leave *Peony* in the hands of her very competent assistant manager. Lila was free to spend her days, and nights, playing with Sam.

Alex and her friends left them in peace. No unannounced visits or off-hours phone calls. She was in touch, in a normal way; as though she didn't have a temporary roommate whom everyone knew shared her bed. She knew Alex wasn't happy with the situation, but she appreciated his backing off. He let her make her own decisions. He acknowledged she was an adult. Lila loved him all the more for it.

They took Cooper for long walks. They found he was a snow dog, happy to frolic for hours. He would chase anything that moved, squirrel, leaf. It was all fair game. Being outdoors with his two favorite people, Cooper was in doggy heaven.

When they returned to the apartment, Cooper collapsed in an exhausted heap, content, and ready to sleep for hours. Lila and Sam used the time to become better acquainted. They would share a quiet meal, discussing a wide variety of topics. Nothing was out of bounds. Politics, religion. Global warming, pollution. *Family Guy* versus *American Dad*. They agreed on most subjects, debated others with a heated respectfulness.

Either way, it always ended the same — in bed. Or on the couch. On the floor. In the shower. The sex was sometimes playful. Sometimes intense. Always satisfying beyond her wildest imagination. Sam was a dream lover. Considerate, inventive, and willing to let Lila experiment. Even when her fantasy turned out to be completely impractical.

"Where did you hear about this position?"

"In a book."

"Not *The Joy of Sex*?" Sam tried to adjust his position. Logistically, Tab A was not going to fit into Slot B.

"No."

Lila shifted. She peered up at him between her spread legs. Bent over, grasping her ankles was an incredibly awkward sex position. Not to mention uncomfortable.

"The *Kama Sutra*?"

"*My Wild Weekend with the Billionaire Next Door.*"

"Ah."

Giving up, Lila straightened. Her only consolation was she could blame her red face on her head being upside down instead of embarrassment. If she was honest, the two were equally to blame.

"Do you often let dubious romance novels guide your sex play?"

"This was the first time," Lila admitted. When Sam began to laugh, she gave him a dirty look. "Hey, it worked for Lance and Angelique."

"Honey, those names alone should give you pause. Lance? As in, his lance thrust into her pleasure hole?"

Lila lost it. She collapsed onto the sofa in a fit of giggles. It wasn't just the words; it was who said them. Sam Laughton, big, bad entertainment mogul spewing horribly dated romance novel euphemisms. If they weren't naked, she would have wished for a camera.

"You need to get with the times, my friend. These days, authors call a spade a spade. Or in this case, a cock a cock."

"Maybe," Sam conceded. "But Lance? Come on."

Hours later, lying in Sam's arms, Lila smiled. He could be so silly. Making her laugh in unexpected ways. Then, on the turn of a dime, he became a focused, passionate lover. At those times, she felt they were the only two people in the world — that she was the only woman he could ever want with such single-minded intensity. If she saw something that wasn't there, she didn't want to know. For the next day and a half, Sam was hers. When he left? Lila mentally shrugged. She refused to miss him before he was gone.

"I can almost hear your mind working," Sam whispered. He nuzzled the side of her neck. "I thought I wore you out. What has you awake when you should be resting up for our next mind-blowing sexual escapades?"

I'm going to miss you. I can't begin to comprehend how much. You've become important. Too important. Who will I talk to late at night? Whose silly jokes will I laugh at? Who will make love to me with white-hot passion, and then hold me as if I'm made of spun glass? And how can I tell you any of this? The answer was simple. She couldn't.

"Lila? Honey? Is something wrong?"

"Yes." Lila wound her arms around Sam's neck. "It's been a whole fifteen minutes since you kissed me."

Sam knew there was more to it. Her tense shoulders, the sadness in her eyes. But he let it go — didn't push. For Lila's sake. And his own.

"A whole fifteen minutes?" Sam rolled her underneath him. "How have you survived?"

Good question, Lila thought. She lifted her mouth, taking Sam's kiss. Savoring. *How would she survive?*

"HELLO, STRANGER. I was wondering if I would see you before you left town."

Sam smiled. Rose yelled the words as she hurried across the street. He took the overflowing canvas bags from her hands.

"Did you cancel tonight's party?"

"No," Rose said. She gave him a friendly kiss on the cheek, efficiently rubbing away the dab of lipstick she'd left behind. "Those bags are full of last minute party necessities. I thought you and Lila might opt out. Word around town is you only venture out to walk the dog."

"Are people saying nasty things about Lila?"

"Of course not," Rose laughed. "She is universally adored. You're both legal and single. The men are jealous. The women are envious. Why would you think otherwise?"

"Harper Falls is a small town."

"Peyton Place." Rose smiled. "You need to update your reading material, Sam."

"That's the second time in the past day someone's told me that."

"Sounds like a story."

Sam shook his head. "A private one."

"Those are the best kind." Rose hooked her arm through his. "Where is the lady in question?"

"She had a shipping snafu to wade through." Sam escorted Rose to her car. "She's meeting me in a few minutes for lunch."

"Any chance you'll be sticking around after tomorrow?"

"No," Sam said firmly. He loaded her bags into the trunk. "Why would you ask?"

"You changed your plans once."

"Rearranged, not changed," Sam corrected. "This is my vacation time. I simply chose to spend it all in Harper Falls."

"With Lila."

"Are you trying to be subtle, Rose?"

"A little," she admitted sheepishly.

"Well, you're lousy at it. If there's something you want to ask, spit it out."

"Okay. Remember you asked for it."

Sam didn't like the glint in Rose's eyes.

"Can I change my mind?"

Rose shook her head. "I only have one question. Are you going to break Lila's heart?"

"Shit."

"I'll take that as a yes."

The condemnation was what set him off. Under normal circumstances, Sam would have easily brushed off Rose's comment. These circumstances were anything *but* normal.

"What about my heart?" he threw out. There was plenty of heat behind his words. Enough to make Rose's eyes widen with surprise.

"I never thought about it."

"Why would you? I'm experienced. Worldly. Lila is sweet. A forgettable Christmas fling."

"Sam —"

"Lila is *not* forgettable, Rose." Frustrated, Sam ran a hand through his hair. "She's bright, funny, beautiful — sexy as hell. I like her. I…"

"You're in love with her," Rose finished for him.

"Is that so hard to believe?"

"Yes."

"I don't know who you're insulting. Me, or Lila."

"You know what I mean, Sam," Rose said. "You are a player. With a big, fat capital P. Admit it, you're as surprised as I am by this turn of events."

Sam couldn't argue.

"Lila is… a revelation." The reverence in his voice was so poignant it brought tears to Rose's eyes.

"Sam Laughton. Who knew you had the soul of a poet." Rose sighed, happy for both her friends. "When are you going to ask her to marry you?"

"I'm not."

"Alex won't like it." Rose shrugged. "Dani will bring him around. A few months without a ring on her finger won't make a difference."

"You don't understand, Rose. I'm not asking her to marry me. Not now. Not ever." Sam cleared his throat. The lump wouldn't move. He was afraid it never would. "When I leave, that's it. I thought I might keep in touch. Visit. But I know that would be a mistake. For both of us."

"Sam." Rose didn't like the look of despair she saw on his face. He stopped at nothing to get what he wanted. Lila loved him, Rose was certain. Why was he walking away from a sure thing?

"It's cold out here, Rose. Go home. I'll see you tonight."

"I'm not budging until you explain this idiocy."

"This is Lila's home, Rose. When she lost her parents, she was drifting — alone." Sam's heart ached when he thought of the tears she shed when she shared her grief. "She has so much here in Harper Falls. A successful business, friends. And most important, her brother. She needs him. She needs all of you. I can't ask her to give it up."

"You picked a hell of a time to get selfless, Sam."

"I've never been in love before."

Rose watched Sam walk away. Love was supposed to be glorious. More often than not, it was just plain hard.

"HAPPY NEW YEAR, Lila."

Lila hugged her brother, grateful once again to have him here. Too many times, she rang in another year with no idea of his whereabouts, or his safety. Knowing that was a thing of the past, helped ease some of the pain she felt. She no longer counted the days until Sam left. Now it was hours and minutes.

"I can still beat the shit out of him for you."

Lila let out a small chuckle. "Sam didn't make me any promises, Alex. I went into this with my eyes wide open."

"I did the same thing when I met Dani." Alex looked across the room at the woman who owned his heart. "I fell in love, knowing I shouldn't. Five years didn't change a damn thing. The second I saw her it could have been five minutes. And I'm an idiot."

"I'm not going to cry," Lila assured her brother. However, it was a close thing. "You don't have to worry about me." Then she did something she had never done before; she lied to her brother's face. "This is a crush, not love. I'll miss Sam for a little while. In a few weeks, he'll be nothing more than a happy memory."

Lila knew Alex didn't believe her. She thought for a moment that he would push her. Thankfully, he let it go. Seeing Sam hold up a glass of champagne, a welcoming smile on his face. Lila willed an answering smile. By the time she reached Sam, she wasn't faking. This was New Year's Eve. A time to celebrate, not mourn.

Wrapping her arms around Sam's neck, Lila gave him a long passionate kiss. They still had a few hours, and she planned on making the most of every second.

"YOU LUCKED OUT on the weather. They're predicting a big snowstorm for tomorrow. Today is clear as a bell."

Lila hated that she was reduced to making small talk. *The weather?* Right now, it was just sad. One more inane comment would topple over into pathetic. It would be nice if Sam would help her out. For the last half hour, his contribution to the conversation amounted to a few grunts followed by the occasional, mmhmm. Was he that anxious to leave that he couldn't be bothered to use actual words?

Lila couldn't complain about their last night together. Cooper was having a sleepover at Rose and Jack's house, so there was no dog to walk. They fell into bed, unable to get enough of each other. So many emotions passed between them. Desperation. Tenderness. The underlying wistfulness couldn't temper the passion or the need to pack as much as possible into these last few precious hours.

Now, with Sam's departure imminent, Lila felt like she watched a stranger pack his bag.

"What are your plans when you get to Los Angeles?"

"Work."

"I know." Lila wanted to shout the words. Instead, she kept her tone light and friendly. "Is there anything specific? We haven't talked about your next project. Is it a movie?"

"Does it matter?"

"Sam. Any second now, I'm going to hit you over the head with the nearest heavy object. Not only will that delay your trip, but I'll be left with a huge mess. Do you know how hard it will be to get blood out of the rug you're standing on?"

When he didn't answer, Lila temper blew.

"Fine. At least do me a favor and move to the right. The kitchen tile is easier to clean."

Lila spun away, tears welling in her eyes. Stupid, stupid man.

"Marry me, Lila."

Sam heard her gasp. She didn't speak or turn. He couldn't see the expression on her face. He was flying blind. After the way he'd acted all morning, it was probably what he deserved.

Neither he nor Lila had a second of sleep the night before. They made the most of every moment. If they weren't making love, they were holding on, pretending the seconds weren't ticking away.

They took one last shower. Came together one more time. Then Sam's brain started working overtime. He heard Lila. He knew she was trying to keep things light. All the time, he was having an argument with himself.

Why couldn't he have Lila? He knew she loved him. She might not see her brother every day, but they could visit. The rest could be worked out later. They belonged together. That was all that mattered.

Blurting out a marriage proposal wasn't the smoothest move he'd ever made, but there it was. As the seconds ticked by, he began to wonder if he'd made a huge miscalculation. Maybe this wasn't what Lila wanted.

"Lila, I know this seems sudden."

"No."

Sam frowned. "No, this isn't sudden?"

"No, I won't marry you."

Sam watched as she turned, stunned to see a huge smile on her face. His world was crumbling around him and she was smiling?

"I see," Sam said stiffly.

"We can't get married, or engaged. Not after a week. When we know each other better, ask me again." She thought for a moment. "On Valentine's day. I'll say yes."

84

Sam swooped Lila into his arms, twirling her around and around until they were both laughing and breathless.

"Wait." Sam pulled back before he could seal it with a kiss. "I have to leave, Lila. There are meetings — business I can't postpone. How are we supposed to get to know each other when we aren't in the same zip code?"

"Tell me you love me."

"Lila."

"Say it, and then I will answer your question."

Sam put his hand under her chin, gently lifting until her eyes met his. His clear blue eyes told her everything. But she still wanted the words.

"I love you, Lila. I know it's been fast, but that doesn't make it any less true. If you'll give me the chance, I will spend every day, for the rest of my life, showing you."

"I swore if the man of my dreams ever told me he loved me, I wouldn't cry." She wiped at the tears on her cheeks. "Just goes to show, you can't plan these things."

"Hey," Sam said, kissing her lightly. "Isn't there something you need to tell me?"

"Right. About our logistics problem."

"Lila."

She loved the way he said her name when he was exasperated. Or when he was happy, or making love with her. She loved everything about him.

"I love you, Sam. A long-distance relationship doesn't cut it for me. So, like it or not, Cooper and I are going with you. Today."

Sam wasn't going to argue. It was exactly what he wanted. He did have a few pertinent questions.

"The shop? Are you okay with leaving *Peony*? Trusting someone else to run your baby?"

"*Peony* has kept me busy, but it isn't my passion or my dream. I want to be a writer, Sam. I want my story published. *If* your contacts think it's good enough."

"I promise to leave the decision in their hands."

What he didn't tell her was his certainty the book would be published. Without any push from him. It was that good. He'd bet anything there would be a bidding war. The sky was the limit. That was something Lila would have the pleasure of finding out when the time came. He wasn't going to spoil the surprise.

"And your brother? Your friends?"

"I will miss seeing them all the time." Lila relaxed in his arms. "Alex will understand. Everyone else will be happy for me. For us."

"Then what are we waiting for?" Sam pushed Lila towards her closet. "Pack your bags, my love. We have a dog to pick up."

Epilogue

LILA'S EYES FLEW open. Eight o'clock? Why was she still in bed on the most important day of her life? Then she remembered. On the night *before* the most important day of her life, Sam did some very creative things with his mouth and a feather duster.

Lila sighed. She floated on a happiness high. One that started on New Year's Day and hadn't waned. Six weeks. A private jet to Los Angeles. Sam's meetings kept them there for several days. Then New York. Broadway, late night suppers. Exclusive designer boutiques — with the *actual* designer present. Finally, Paris. Home.

Lila threw back the covers. A shower in the luxurious bathroom was what she needed. She slipped from the bed, pausing at the window. The neighborhood was one of the most exclusive in Paris. They were somewhere over the Atlantic Ocean when Sam mentioned the location of his apartment. Saint Germain-des-Prés. Lila quickly looked it up. Holy crap.

"Sam?" Lila asked in a hushed tone.

"Yes?"

Sam, reclining in one of the plane's cushy chairs, put the script he was reading on a pile of six or seven others. Potential future projects. Though nothing was catching his interest.

Lila's eyes were as wide as saucers. Through this entire whirlwind, she tried to maintain an even keel. Impressed, but not gushing. She didn't want Sam to think he'd saddled himself with an unsophisticated twit. This was too much. How could you maintain a blasé attitude when your future home was not only in Paris but on the Seine?

"Do you know where you live?"

"Where *we* live," Sam corrected. "And yes, I'm acquainted with the area."

"Oscar Wilde and Cole Porter lived there." Lila bounced up, bursting with excitement. "Paris, Sam. I'm in love and going to live in Paris."

"Finally." Sam snagged Lila around the waist, pulling her onto his lap. "I was wondering what it would take to strip away that ridiculous veneer of sophistication you put up."

"You knew I was faking?" Lila frowned. "Why didn't you say anything?"

"Honey." Sam kissed her cheek. "Everything happened so fast. If you needed to put on a temporary mask out in public while you adjusted, I was fine with that. As long as you were you in private, I had no complaints."

"I was afraid if I ran around all wide-eyed, asking questions. Pointing at one thing after another, you might dump me back in Harper Falls and find yourself a woman less inclined to gawk."

"Never again," Sam said sternly. "Don't hide yourself from me, Lila. I love your enthusiasm. I'm looking forward to showing you Paris. I want to see it again for the first time with you — through your eyes."

"Be careful what you ask for," Lila warned. She relaxed, perhaps for the first time since leaving Harper Falls. "I want to see everything."

And that's what she did. When Sam wasn't working, he walked with her. The rest of the time, Lila was happy to wander Paris on her own. It would take years, decades, to see it all. She could hardly wait.

After a quick shower, Lila threw on a pair of jeans, a burgundy sweater, and thick socks. Paris in February was damp and chilly. Then she went looking for her men.

"Sam? Cooper?"

No response. Maybe they were out for their morning run. Cooper was adjusting to his new lifestyle beautifully. You would think he was born to city life. Maybe he was? They didn't know. But he belonged to them now, and they belonged to him. She, Sam, and Cooper. A very happy family.

Smelling coffee, Lila walked to the kitchen. Sam enlarged the area before he moved in. He managed to keep the Parisian feel while updating it to fit his modern tastes. She reached for a mug when she heard the front door open.

"Hey," she called out. "I was wondering where you were."

Lila looked in the living room, a smile of greeting on her face. Cooper sat alone in the middle of the room, smiling back.

"I know you're talented, but you did not come in by yourself."

Lila knelt, patting Cooper's head. Suddenly, she noticed the red, silk ribbon tied around his neck.

"What's this?"

Making a closer examination, Lila ran her hand over the ribbon. She froze when she felt the circle of metal. A ring.

"It's Valentine's Day."

"That's what the calendar says."

Sam. Lila's heart skipped a beat. She couldn't believe he was hers. Gorgeous, sexy. Blue eyes to die for. Kind. Not perfect, but perfect for her.

Sam took the ribbon, letting the ring fall into his hand.

"I know you better than I did six weeks ago," he began. "I hope to spend the rest of my life growing with you, changing. Doing my best to make you happy. Loving you. Marry me, Lila. Please?"

Sam Laughton. The man helped her make her dreams come true. What else could she say?

"Yes."

###

www.ingramcontent.com/pod-product-compliance
Lightning Source LLC
Chambersburg PA
CBHW071339130626
46556CB00004B/1947